A Sparkling New Case . . .

"The International Diamond Jewelry Show and Auction is scheduled to run at the convention center this coming weekend," Q explained. *"It will feature several pieces valued at over ten million dollars apiece, with a total value upward of two hundred million. What's more, the jewels will be worn by a pair of well-known supermodels whom . . . ahem . . . I'm sure you've heard of: Naomi Dowd and Shakira."*

I looked over at Joe, who looked back at me with a smile so big you'd think he just won one of those diamonds.

"The reason we've brought you in is that Interpol has intercepted some very troubling e-mail communications indicating that there may be an attempt to steal some, or even all, of the jewels at the show."

"And there's our cue," Joe said.

THE HARDY BOYS

UNDERCOVER BROTHERS™

Available from Simon & Schuster

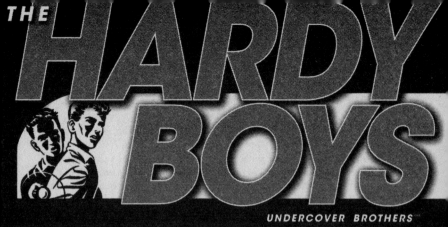

THE HARDY BOYS

UNDERCOVER BROTHERS™

#15 **Death and Diamonds**

FRANKLIN W. DIXON

Aladdin Paperbacks
New York   London   Toronto   Sydney

☛ ALADDIN PAPERBACKS
An imprint of Simon & Schuster
Children's Publishing Division
1230 Avenue of the Americas
New York, NY 10020

Copyright © 2007 by Simon & Schuster, Inc.

THE HARDY BOYS MYSTERY STORIES and HARDY BOYS UNDER-COVER BROTHERS are trademarks of Simon & Schuster, Inc.
ALADDIN PAPERBACKS and colophon are trademarks of Simon & Schuster, Inc.
Designed by Lisa Vega
The text of this book was set in Aldine 401BT.
Manufactured in the United States of America
First Aladdin Paperbacks edition April 2007
20 19 18 17 16 15 14 13 12 11

Library of Congress Control Number 2006934562
ISBN-13: 978-1-4169-3402-8
ISBN-10: 1-4169-3402-2
0512 OFF

TABLE OF CONTENTS

FRANK

1.

April in Paris

I'd seen Paris before, but only in postcards. This time I was getting a close-up view of the Eiffel Tower. Really close—I was dangling from it by my fingernails! Only a pair of high-tech gloves, with highly magnetized finger pads, kept me from falling four hundred feet to the ground.

Climbing just above me were a couple of guys who'd stolen a pair of paintings from the Louvre, France's most famous museum. Those priceless works of art were now rolled up inside cardboard tubes strapped to their backs—but my brother, Joe, and I were more worried about the semiautomatic pistols they were firing down at us.

How did we wind up in this position?

It's a long story. I'll just say that everything that

could have gone wrong did go wrong. Still, we'd managed to catch up to these two guys. Now we were just about to bring them to justice—except they had guns, and we didn't.

On the other hand, we did have those excellent magnetized gloves. Very cutting edge. Joe and I were asked to try them out by ATAC (American Teens Against Crime), the top secret organization that was founded by our dad, Fenton Hardy, to catch criminals older crime fighters might not be able to get to.

Anyway—back to dangling from the tower.

"We've got 'em cornered now, Joe!" I shouted. "They're running out of real estate."

"Frank!" Joe yelled back, staring past me. "Chopper at two o'clock!"

I looked over my shoulder. Out of the clear night sky, the lights and noise of a helicopter were coming straight for us. I had the sinking feeling it wasn't here to help us out.

We *had* called the gendarmes—that's the French police—earlier, while chasing our quarry through the streets of Paris's Latin Quarter. But neither of us speaks French very well, and if the gendarmes spoke any English, they weren't telling.

By the time we'd started climbing the tower, it was too late. My cell phone batteries were dead.

Joe had dropped his cell while putting on those magnetic gloves, and he hadn't realized it until we were halfway up the tower.

So I could only assume that the chopper was here to evacuate those two cornered bad guys—and finish me and Joe off in the process.

The thieves were nearing the top of the tower. True, they didn't have our gloves, but they did have steel cables and carabiners—the same ones they'd used to rappel down through the skylights of the museum and steal the paintings. With the help of those cables, and the suction cups at the ends of them, they were climbing the steel beams one at a time, just fast enough to stay ahead of us.

They'd already reached the observation deck— conveniently closed for renovations—and were making their way to the needle at the top of the tower. There, I could only assume that the helicopter would pick them up and scoot them off to safety.

If their plan succeeded, those two precious paintings would never be seen again—except by whichever evil multimillionaire had paid for the heist.

A bullet pinged off the beam just to the right of my head, sending sparks flying.

Yikes!

(Stupid. But what would *you* say if you were almost hit by a bullet?)

I swung myself to the inside of the beam, where it was easier to hide—but harder to climb.

Joe, younger than me by a year but stronger by a lot, was at least twenty feet above me by now. He was perched just under the observation deck, in even greater danger than I was.

The helicopter had reached the tower and was now hovering only a few dozen feet over the needle. A cable was lowered slowly downward from the chopper, and the thieves started reaching out to grab it.

I knew this was our last chance, and so did Joe. While their focus was on grabbing the cable, they wouldn't be paying attention to us.

Climbing as fast as I could, I closed the distance between us, catching up to Joe alongside the observation deck.

"You still got that titanium apparatus?" he asked me.

"Uh-huh." I showed him the contraption strapped to my left forearm. It contained a spool of thin but superstrong titanium cable with a sharp grappling hook at the end.

"Now would be an excellent time to use it."

Like I needed to be told.

Aiming my arm at the narrow spot on the chopper—right behind the side opening, and just in front of the tail—I pressed the trigger and shot the bolt.

With a soft whoosh, the cable rocketed outward. It wound itself around the chopper's landing gear three or four times before the hook grabbed hold.

I tugged on the cable to see if it was secure, then gave Joe a nod. He hooked both arms around me from behind. "Go! Go! Go!"

We let go of the steel beams, swinging free just as the two bad guys were climbing into the chopper.

Not a moment too soon, either. With the two men safely aboard, the helicopter banked hard right and flew off into the night—unknowingly trailing Joe and me behind it.

I pushed the button on the cable apparatus. It started winding itself back up—and in the process, lifting us toward the helicopter. What with our combined weight and the pull from the speeding chopper, it felt like my left arm was being pulled out of its socket, but somehow I held on as we got in range of the chopper's side opening.

I pushed the cable's stop button when we were close enough to the landing gear to grab hold of it.

"Got it!" Joe yelled, and let go of me. I glanced over, just in time to see him disappear into the chopper.

Good. He'd obviously taken them by surprise, or they would have tossed him right back overboard. Hopefully, he could keep them busy long enough for me to get on board as well.

I hoisted myself up and rolled over into the chopper.

Instantly I sized up the situation. Joe was on his back, with both bad guys standing over him. One was pointing a gun at his face. I grabbed that guy by the ankle and yanked him off his feet. Then I ducked the punch the other thug was throwing at me. He missed so badly he fell on the floor—and rolled right into his buddy, who was getting up. The impact sent the second guy stumbling. He reached for the wall of the chopper—but there was no wall. He was right at the opening. The next thing any of us knew, he was gone!

All three of us stared at the opening where he'd disappeared. Then we looked at one another, knowing that one false move and we could easily follow him.

Man, what a way to go. I sure hoped he didn't hit anyone on the ground when he landed.

Joe and I both jumped the remaining thug. With the two of us working together, it wasn't much of a contest—Joe wound up knocking him out with his own pistol.

"Nice work!" I said as he dragged the limp body out of harm's way.

A thought suddenly hit me. It was amazing that the pilot hadn't yet realized what was going on behind him.

Too amazing. Turning toward the cockpit, I saw him leveling a huge machine gun at us.

"Duck!" Joe yelled.

I hit the ground as the bullets flew. Luckily, the recoil pushed the pilot back into his instruments. That made the chopper start veering madly to the left, then right. All of us went tumbling back and forth, out of control.

Joe dragged himself forward along the floor with the help of his magnetic gloves. Soon he and the pilot were locked in a death struggle, fighting over the machine gun between them.

I had no gun, but with them fighting, and the other guy out cold, my path to the cockpit was clear.

I'd never flown a chopper before, but I *had* flown several different kinds of small planes. With a little trial and error (well, more than a little) I was finally able to figure out the stabilizers and rotor controls and pull us out of our death spiral in time to save the day.

I looked back into the cabin to see Joe, with the machine gun slung over his shoulder, standing over the unconscious pilot.

"Got any twine up there?" he shouted over the noise. "I think I should tie these two together, just in case."

I smiled, and he smiled back. I didn't have any twine, but it didn't matter. The Eiffel Tower was just below us. I lowered the chopper onto the adjoining field, the Champ de Mars, and cut the engine.

We stepped out of the helicopter to find a squadron of gendarmes waiting for us. I handed them the tubes containing the two priceless paintings, saying a few of the French words I knew: *"Bonsoir, mes amis."* Hey, I try.

One of them said something in French that I couldn't understand, shook our hands, and ordered the others to take the bad guys into custody. They shoved them into a paddy wagon and took off, waving good-bye and leaving us standing there like a couple of beat-up morons.

"That's all the thanks we get?" Joe asked, amazed.

"Hey," I said, "I'm sure they're grateful—they're just . . . busy."

"Man," Joe said, shaking his head, "I could use a hot bath and a good hot meal. How 'bout you?"

"Oui, oui," I said, working my French a little more to make the most of my last hours in the country. "And as you know, *mon frère*, this town has the best food in the entire universe."

"Uh-huh," Joe said, clearly more interested in food than in French. "Let's do it."

JOE

2.

Dream On

It was wicked hot for late April, almost like summer—which only added to our lazy attitudes. I had a bad case of jet lag, but Frank's was even worse.

We were both sitting out in our backyard, back in Bayport, USA, sipping cold lemonades brought to us by good old Aunt Trudy.

"I hope you boys realize school starts up again on Monday," Trudy said.

"Aaark! School boys! School boys!" This from Playback, our pet parrot—or should I say *Aunt Trudy's* pet parrot. He's never far from her shoulder, and he's *always* got something to say—usually something annoying.

"What day is it?" Frank asked, shielding his face from the sun with the newspaper.

"It's Saturday, of course," said Aunt Trudy, clucking her tongue. "You two act as if you'd been running a marathon, not spending a week's vacation in Paris."

"Some vacation," Frank muttered, and I had to agree. I was sore from head to toe, even after a last-minute visit to the hot tub in our Paris hotel.

"I declare," said Trudy, grabbing the tray and starting back toward the kitchen, "you boys are the laziest people I know."

"Lazy! Lazy!" Playback screeched.

I thought about dousing Playback with my lemonade, but I didn't want to get Aunt Trudy wet.

"Joe?" Frank said when Trudy and Playback were gone. "Did you check out this headline?"

"What headline?"

He showed me as he read, "'French Police Nab Notorious Art Theft Ring.'"

"Does it mention us?" I asked.

"Of course not. And don't go blaming the gendarmes. You know ATAC is allergic to publicity. If we cared about getting famous, we should have set up in business for ourselves."

"Hmmm," I said. "Sounds good to me. I'm sick of other people taking all the credit."

"You know, Joe, fame's not all it's cracked up to be," Frank said. "Look at how miserable all those movie stars, famous athletes, and supermodels are."

"According to whom?"

"According to all those magazines you like to look at in the supermarket checkout line."

I just rolled my eyes.

"Hey, speaking of supermodels, here's something closer to home," Frank said, suddenly sitting up and looking more awake than he had in the past three days. "Get this: 'Big Diamond Jewelry Show and Auction at New Bayport Convention Center Will Feature Naomi Dowd.'"

"*Naomi Dowd*? In *Bayport*?" I said, getting to my feet.

In case you just arrived from Mars, Naomi Dowd is possibly the hottest supermodel alive. Blond, blue eyes, full lips . . .

"We are so *there*, dude," I said.

"I'm afraid not," Frank said. "Cool your jets, Joe—this show's by invitation only."

"So how do we get an invite?"

"We don't—it's for industry reps, buyers, jewelers— you know. And it says here that the jewelry on display—diamonds, mostly—is expected to fetch over twenty million dollars."

"Let me see that." I grabbed the paper from him. "Hey!"

"Let's see . . . ah, here we go . . . 'Up-and-coming

supermodel Shakira will also be wearing the fabulous creations by world-class jewelry designers.'" I thought for a second. "Shakira—isn't she the one who was on the cover of the swimsuit issue?"

"Yeah. There's a picture of her on the other page."

I turned the page, and sure enough, it was her—dark hair, copper skin, exotic as they come. "Man, she's even more gorgeous than Naomi!"

Just my type.

Okay, Naomi Dowd is *also* my type. When it comes to supermodels, I'm not picky.

"We've *got* to get an invitation, Frank," I said. "This is too good, and too close to home to miss!"

"Dream on," he said. "Me, I'm going upstairs to take a nap."

He left me there with the *Bayport Times* and my lemonade. I sat back in my lounge chair, thinking about whom I'd rather date—Naomi Dowd or Shakira. It was a hard choice.

I was just going over the two of them in my mind's eye, when I heard the window above me shatter.

I immediately covered my face with the paper to protect it from any falling shards of glass. "What the—?"

I ran to the garden fence, just in time to see the bratty kid who'd thrown the rock jumping over the neighbor's fence, and racing off on his bicycle.

I made it to the garage in no time flat, revved up my motorcycle, and started muttering under my breath. "That kid is going to pay! Who does he think he is?"

I hadn't been for a ride in weeks, and I could hear that the bike's engine needed a tune-up. It was misfiring badly, so I shut it off and tried Frank's instead.

I wasn't worried about the kid on the bicycle getting a head start. Our motorcycles have enough power to catch a race car, let alone a ten-speed. By the way, they're also tricked out like nobody's business with every awesome feature you could ever dream of—not because we're brats, mind you. We use our bikes in crime fighting all the time, so we've *got* to have the latest and greatest technology.

The fact that they're also mad fun has absolutely nothing to do with it.

Anyway, I was just pulling out of the garage and into the driveway when Frank caught up to me. "Hey, Joe!" he yelled. "Wait!"

I held up my hand and tried to explain. "Mine needs a tune-up," I said. "Don't worry, I'll bring it back as soon as I've dusted off that jerk who threw the rock through your window."

"That's what I'm trying to tell you!" Frank said. "It wasn't a rock!"

"Huh?"

He held up a package. It was addressed "Frank and Joe Hardy—open immediately, *FYEO*." (That means "For Your Eyes Only"—but you knew that 'cause of James Bond, right?)

"Are you kidding me?" I said, shutting off the bike's engine.

"Nope. It's gotta be from ATAC."

I shook my head in amazement. "You know, just once, those guys could deliver our next case in the regular mail."

3.
An Engraved Invitation

We raced back into the house and up the stairs, passing Aunt Trudy and Playback on the way. "My goodness!" she said, backing up against the wall. "What woke you two up?"

Apparently she hadn't heard the glass of Frank's bedroom window shattering. Probably because Playback was squawking in her ear.

"No worries, Aunt Trudy," I said, running past her.

We locked the door of Frank's room behind us and ripped open the package. Inside it we found a video game CD labeled "Deadly Diamonds."

Joe and I looked at each other. "Are you thinking what I'm thinking?" he said.

"Nah, that would be too good to be true," I said,

popping the CD into our video game system and flicking on the monitor.

The machine booted up, and while it did, I examined the rest of the package. There wasn't much inside—none of the usual extra cash, credit cards, or high-tech gadgets we usually get at the beginning of a case. Just two laminated passes with our names and pictures on them, marked CONVENTION CENTER SECURITY: ACCESS ALL AREAS.

Convention center? Could it really be…?

Sure enough, a wide shot of the brand-new Bayport Convention Center flashed on the monitor's screen, accompanied by the soothing, mellow voice of Q, our boss at ATAC.

"Hello, Frank and Joe," he said, *"and welcome back from your successful stay in Paris. Sorry to bother you again on such short notice, but I'm afraid something's come up, and you're the nearest agents to hand.*

"I'm sure that, as natives of Bayport, you're familiar with the marvelous new convention center that opened in January. I don't know if you've been there before, but if not, you're going to get your chance now."

The picture on the screen changed to a montage shot of tons of diamonds. We saw diamonds in the rough, diamonds after being cut, diamonds set in gold, on necklaces and bracelets, in earrings and engagement rings and belly-button rings. *Big* diamonds. Some as big as the thumb of the person holding it for the picture.

"*The International Diamond Jewelry Show and Auction is scheduled to run at the convention center this coming weekend,*" Q explained. "*It will feature several pieces valued at over ten million dollars apiece, with a total value upwards of two hundred million. What's more, the jewels will be worn by a pair of well-known supermodels whom . . . ahem . . . I'm sure you've heard of: Naomi Dowd and Shakira.*"

I looked over at Joe, who looked back at me with a smile so big you'd think he'd just won one of those diamonds.

"*The reason we've brought you in is that Interpol has intercepted some very troubling e-mail communications indicating that there may be an attempt to steal some, or even all, of the jewels at the show.*"

"And there's our cue," Joe said.

"*Seeing how the models involved are only slightly older than yourselves,*" Q continued, "*and how you're conveniently located right there in Bayport, we at ATAC thought it would be prudent to place you on the inside, with the job of shadowing the two models. I'm . . . ahem . . . sure you won't object when I tell you that you're to stick with them as closely as possible. To that end, we've issued you full-clearance security passes, as you've no doubt already discovered.*"

"No doubt," Joe echoed, fingering his pass lovingly.

"And now," Q continued, *"let me give you a little background on the e-mails we've received, and on the diamonds in question. First, the diamonds: They are part of an illegal shipment captured last year by Interpol agents as they were being sent to Antwerp, the world's major center for diamond cutting and selling. The shipment was traced back to the Philippine island of Jolo, home base of a guerrilla/terrorist movement led by a warlord named Carlos Sanguillen."*

"Never heard of him," Joe said.

"Shhh," I said. "Just listen, will you?"

"Sanguillen is known for his brutal tactics—murder of innocent civilians, terror, kidnappings—and for using illegally mined diamonds to finance his operations. We know the diamonds in question were illegally mined, because they lacked the identifying numbers micro-etched in all legal diamonds worldwide since 2004. These identifying numbers are invisible to the naked eye, but can be quite plainly seen under any household microscope.

"Having taken possession of the diamonds, Interpol decided to have them fashioned into jewelry by some of the world's leading designers and auctioned off at a high-profile show, with all proceeds going to benefit the victims of Sanguillen's terror. That show is the one you'll be attending, boys. All for a good cause, as it were."

"But?" Joe prompted.

"But," Q responded, *"that brings us to the e-mails. They were intercepted over the last three weeks, beginning the day after the Bayport Convention Center was chosen for the show. They indicate that mobsters based in Atlantic City, New Jersey—and specifically a high-ranking mobster by the name of Shakey Twist—may be planning to pull off a spectacular heist at the show itself."*

The screen showed the mug shot of a truly vile-looking guy, with a pencil-thin mustache, a scar across his left cheek, and a snarling expression that made us lean back, away from the screen.

"Twist has been tried for murder six times, for grand larceny over a dozen times, and for various other offenses as well, but he has never been convicted of anything more serious than jaywalking. Obviously, he has ways of swaying juries—or even judges—that we haven't been able to pinpoint."

The picture of Twist was replaced by that of another thuggish-looking guy, this one darker skinned, more heavily mustached, and even more evil looking, if that was possible. The caption under his face read: "Carlos Sanguillen."

"The e-mails also indicate that Sanguillen himself may be a part of the plot. Interpol was tracking his movements until last week, when they lost him at the airport in Antwerp. They're afraid, and so are we, that both he and

Twist may show up in Bayport on the day of the show, with lots of heavily armed backup.

"Naturally, security will be as tight as a drum. The convention center's perimeter will be guarded by dozens of security personnel, including FBI, Bayport police, and private security guards.

"And the convention center's security is also top-notch. When you arrive there on the morning of the show next Saturday, you'll be given a complete tour of their systems by the security chief, Hal Harris. He's already been advised of your presence and told to keep your association with ATAC to himself. Let's hope he does."

"Definitely," I said. Letting word slip that we were with ATAC was *not* an option.

"Naturally, there'll be a large, well-off audience present at the convention center to bid on the jewelry pieces," Q went on. "Be aware, boys, that they, too, may present a tempting target for the likes of Twist, Sanguillen, and their henchmen—whose identities are largely still unknown to us.

"What we're most afraid of is that this will be an inside job. And that's where you two come in. Your assignment: Uncover the plot and prevent the theft before it happens— and while you're at it, keep those two supermodels safe from harm."

"Yessir!" Joe said, saluting the screen with a great big smile.

"As usual," Q finished, *"this CD will self-erase in five seconds. Good luck, boys."*

There was a hissing sound, and the screen went blank. Q's voice was replaced with a blaring song by Freaks of Nature, one of our favorite bands.

"Warlords? Diamonds? Supermodels?" Joe shouted over the blasting music. "Dude, we are *so* there!"

4.
We Take the Grand Tour

It was a really hard week at school. It was hard to concentrate knowing that in a few days we'd be hanging out with Naomi Dowd and Shakira. I just about flunked a history test, and Frank didn't do much better. Good thing it wasn't finals week.

The worst part was, we couldn't talk about any of it to anyone—not even our best friends! (When I say that ATAC is supersecret, I do mean supersecret.) But our friends Chet and Iola knew something was up by the way we were acting. Usually Frank and I are pretty chill, but that week we were like a pair of Mexican jumping beans.

I got a really expensive haircut on Friday afternoon, so that I'd look good for our crime fighting.

Normally I didn't care, but . . . okay, I always care. But this time it was really important!

As I lay in bed Friday night, I couldn't help imagining what it would be like, meeting and hanging out with a pair of supermodels. I couldn't decide which one was more gorgeous—Naomi or Shakira.

I tried to picture myself taking one or the other of them out to dinner, but I couldn't see it—me, sitting across the table from Naomi, or reaching across it to take Shakira's hand, gazing into their gorgeous eyes? I wouldn't know what to say!

Finally I got to sleep—only to be jerked awake by my insanely annoying alarm at 10 a.m. I got up, hit the alarm clock until it stopped, and checked myself out in the mirror.

Oh, no—was that a *zit* coming on? It *couldn't* be! Not now!

This was so unlike me. Usually, it's Frank who makes a geek out of himself over pretty girls—but then, Naomi Dowd and Shakira were not just your average girls next door.

I smacked myself on both sides of the face, saying, "Get a grip, Joe," into the mirror. Then I took a shower, got dressed, and went downstairs.

Aunt Trudy was there, hovering over Frank, who was sitting at the breakfast table looking tired and glum. "I don't know what's the matter with your brother," she said to me. "He usually has such a good appetite in the mornings."

"I'm not hungry either." It was true—I couldn't have held food down if I tried. I was *way* too nervous.

"My goodness!" Trudy said. "I think you two had better see the doctor—I can't ever remember you *both* being uninterested in food."

"Is Dad up yet?" I asked.

"He had to go out early this morning," Aunt Trudy said. "Something about that show over at the convention center."

So Dad was involved too. That meant the police were expecting big trouble.

"And your mother's off at the library, doing inventory."

Our mom is the head of the Bayport library system—she's supersmart and knows a lot about a million different subjects. But she knows nothing about our involvement with ATAC, and neither does Aunt Trudy. Just Dad.

"Well, we'd better be going," Frank said, getting up from the table. "Joe? Ready?"

"Ready as I'll ever be," I answered.

"And where are you two off to?" Aunt Trudy asked.

"We're going to see the show at the convention

center, Aunt Trudy," Frank explained. "It's the biggest thing to hit Bayport in years, haven't you heard?"

He gave her a smile and a quick peck on the cheek, and Trudy calmed down. I had to hand it to him—the man was slick.

"Liar, liar, pants on fire!" Playback shouted after him as we left. "Pretty bird! Pretty bird!"

Playback, apparently, wasn't feeling as calm as Trudy.

Frank gritted his teeth. "How does he always know?" he asked me as we hit the garage and got on Frank's bike. I had to ride with him, because I'd brought mine to the shop for a quick, morning tune-up.

"Maybe he reads the paper when you're not looking," I said.

"You know," he said, gunning the engine, "I wouldn't be the least bit surprised."

The Bayport Convention Center was designed by a world-famous architect. It's awesome. It looks like this shining metal meteorite sitting on the edge of the bay. Since it opened up, it's been booked with one big convention or show after another.

But this diamond show to benefit the victims of violence in the Third World was the biggest event yet, by far. The number of security personnel ring-ing the convention center made that obvious the minute we got within half a mile.

I recognized Chief Ezra Collig, head of the Bayport Police Department, directing his officers to positions at key intersections. And there was our dad, standing right next to him.

"Yo, Frank," I said into his ear, "let's take a detour."

He nodded in agreement, and we took a left, heading down to the bay before veering around the other side of the half-mile-long building. Neither one of us wanted to have to explain to the chief what we were doing there. I figured he'd spot us eventually, but I hoped we'd be well along in our investigation by that time.

The chief knows about our involvement with ATAC, and he's usually pretty good about helping us. But when it came to something as big as this show—and on his own turf, no less—we both knew he wouldn't want to let us anywhere near the convention center. He'd probably get annoyed that ATAC didn't ask his permission before assigning us to the case.

But I understood why they wouldn't. These were big organized crime groups we were talking about. Big enough to have a man on the inside of a local security operation, or even the police force.

Frank and I parked his bike at the nearby marina and ran up the front steps of the convention center. In the lobby, we walked over to the information booth. "We're looking for the head of security," I said.

She looked me and Frank up and down, giving us the once-over. "That would be Mr. Harris," she said, nodding over to the far end of the gigantic, glass-walled lobby, where a tall, thin man with a lion's mane of white hair was barking orders into a walkie-talkie.

We headed in his direction. "Are you Mr. Harris?" Frank asked him.

"That's me. And you are?"

"Frank Hardy, sir. And this is my brother, Joe."

"Ah, yes . . . we've been expecting you," he said, shaking our hands. "You're the ones who are going to be keeping an eye on our models, eh? Lucky fellows. Well, let me give you the tour of our operations—starting with the control room. Follow me, please."

He led us to a private elevator, and we rode up to a glass-walled enclosure overlooking the lobby on one side, and the main hall of the convention center on the other. In the middle of the control room was a bank of monitors, showing live pictures of every corner of the center, inside and out, in quick succession.

"Every one of these monitors will be manned from two o'clock this afternoon on," he said. "There's no way anyone will be able to approach the merchandise without our knowing about it."

"How many cameras in all?" Frank asked.

"Seventy-two," said Harris. "And that's just to cover the inside. There are another sixty mounted on trucks outside the building."

"Very impressive," I said.

"Oh, that's just the start of it," he said. "Come on, I'll show you the rest." He walked up to one of the glass walls and placed his palm on a heat-sensitive ceramic pad. Lights flashed green, and a sliding panel opened to reveal a secure hallway. "This way, boys."

The hallway led us above the main hall, which we could see through the glass floor of the corridor as well as through the walls. "It's all one-way glass," Harris said proudly. "Everything here is the last word in secure design. When you want to attract the biggest, most expensive shows, you can't offer anything less."

We reached another door, with another ceramic panel. Once again, he placed his palm against it, and it opened to reveal yet another elevator. We rode this one down, right past the floor of the main hall and into the basement.

"Now I'll show you where the gems will be brought in and kept until it's time for them to be shown off."

We followed him down a long corridor, turning left, then right, then left again. Noticing air shafts along the ceiling, I cleared my throat, pointing upward. "Um, what about those, sir?"

"Very observant," said Harris. "Don't worry, the police have those covered at all access points."

I nodded, but once his eyes were off me, I shot Frank a worried glance and saw that he wasn't convinced either. If this was the mob we were talking about, they had ways to get around even the most airtight security systems.

We came to another door, with another ceramic identification panel. On the other side of this door was a large hall with a high, airy ceiling, with natural light pouring in through thick glass-brick skylights.

In the middle of the hall were a number of pedestals with glass boxes on top. The boxes were empty, but I could tell they wouldn't be for long.

Standing in front of one of the boxes was a brown-haired guy wearing a very expensive suit and tie. His yearly manicure bills were probably as much as my dad's salary. Harris shook his hand, then introduced him to us.

"Frank and Joe Hardy, meet Vincent Carrera, the promoter of tonight's show." Turning to Carrera, he added, "The Hardys are here to provide extra undercover security for Naomi and Shakira."

"Ah. Excellent," said Carrera, in a heavy, upper-crust European accent. "So pleased to meet you both."

We all shook hands, and then Harris said, "I've just been giving them the grand tour of the convention center's security systems. But perhaps you'd like to tell them about the 'treasure room.'" He turned back to us. "This," he said, gesturing at the hall around us, "is the treasure room."

"Yes," Carrera said, giving us all a patient smile. "The spot where we're now standing is at ground zero, so to speak, of the convention center's security. If the systems were turned on, we'd all be covered from head to toe by laser motion detectors linked to all the convention center's alarm systems. If we were thieves, we'd have maybe ten seconds before we were surrounded by heavily armed security personnel."

Harris beamed, as if he were the proud parent of a bouncing baby being shown off to admiring relatives for the first time.

"These glass boxes," Carrera continued, "are where the diamond jewelry will be stored when it arrives."

"When will that be?" I asked.

He checked his watch. "Any moment now, as a matter of fact. And here they will remain until Naomi and Shakira place them around their pretty necks and arms."

He placed a hand on one of the glass boxes. "These are not made of ordinary glass, either. Oh, no. The glass is backed by plastic so tough it would take a well-muscled weight lifter over half an hour to smash through it with a hammer. By that time, of course," he added with that patient smile, "we'd have him safely in irons."

These two guys seemed to me to be overly confident in their preventive measures. In my experience, it pays to never underestimate the bad guys. You never know what surprises they've got up their sleeves. After all, they get to make the first move. Not that the security measures weren't impressive— it was Harris's and Carrera's overconfidence that bothered me.

But who was I to say anything yet? These two were the ones in charge. Frank and I were only here to make sure the models were safe, and that the jewels weren't stolen from off their bodies. That much, I thought we could handle.

Carrera's walkie-talkie chirped, and he answered

it. "Yes? Ah, excellent. We're all ready down here. Make sure the police are in position first."

Hanging up, he turned to us. "The diamonds have arrived. If you'd like, you can stay and watch as they're brought in and certified."

It took a while for them to get to the hall where we were stationed, so Frank and I spent the meantime surveying the laser motion detectors and the silent alarm systems, all of them coded and interconnected.

Everything seemed secure, I had to admit. But professional thieves—especially the mob—are very well educated in this sort of high-tech security. Their whole operation depends on staying one step ahead of the good guys.

I was pretty sure, given the intercepted e-mails, that they would take a stab at stealing the diamonds, security or no security.

The gems arrived, along with about a dozen Bayport police and a very efficient-looking man with a leather briefcase. "This is Mr. Nicholas Edmondson, our local gemological expert," Carrera told us. "Mr. Edmondson, this is Mr. Harris, head of security for the convention center—and these are the personal undercover security guards for the models."

"Frank and Joe Hardy," Frank said helpfully, nodding in Edmondson's direction.

Case by heavy steel case, Carrera lifted the diamond jewelry out, held them up for us to see, and then handed them to Edmondson, who looked each item over closely with a special high-magnification eyepiece. "Each gem has a microscopic identifying number etched on it with a laser," Carrera explained.

"Yes, this is authentic," Mr. Edmondson said after viewing each piece in turn. "And the number matches. Beautiful . . . just beautiful . . ."

I've got to say, the jewels *were* spectacular—necklaces with diamonds as big as Ping-Pong balls; bracelets so thick with glittering diamonds that I had to shade my eyes; earrings so big and heavy I wondered if Naomi's and Shakira's earlobes would get stretched out by them.

It took about twenty minutes for Edmondson to certify them all, and for Carrera to load them into their display cases. Then Harris went over to the far side of the hall and keyed in a code number. Suddenly there was a soft humming noise.

Harris smiled. "The bottoms of the glass cubes are magnetized to hold them firmly in place. I'm the only one who knows the code to release the magnetic locks. During the show, I will come down here and release them, one at a time, so that the models can put the jewels on—and afterward, I'll lock them right back down again."

"Well," said Carrera, "I think we're finished here for the moment. Time to go, everybody."

"Um, I don't mean to be a pain," I said, "but shouldn't someone stay here with the gems at all times?"

Carrera gave me his most patient smile. "That won't be necessary," he said. "The Bayport police have a tight cordon around the entire convention center, and all security personnel have been vetted by Mr. Harris. Besides, the closed-circuit cameras and motion-sensing laser alarms are all on. I think the gems will be safest if they're left alone until showtime."

I shrugged. "Whatever."

We were about to follow them out of the hall when Chief Collig met us at the door, accompanied by Officer Con Reilly, one of dad's old friends on the force.

"Well, look who's here!" said the chief—meaning me and Frank. I could tell by his frown that he wasn't pleased.

"We've been hired on as extra security," Frank explained quickly.

"Oh, is that so?" said the chief. "And by whom?"

"Um . . . by our dad," said Frank, giving the chief a meaningful look. Even though Chief Collig and Hal Harris knew about ATAC, none of the other guys in the room did, and it was important that they didn't find out. As I've said before, ATAC is a top secret organization, and it's vital that it stay that way, no matter what.

"Ah . . . yes, of course," said the chief, getting the message. He turned to the others. "Their dad is an ex-cop, and a good one too—Fenton Hardy. He still . . . er . . . does some consulting for us."

"I see," said Harris, pleased to see that the chief of the Bayport Police Department was okay with our being there.

Carrera's walkie-talkie chirped again. "Yes? Ah, wonderful! We'll be right up to meet her!" He gave us all a big, wide smile—not at all like the fake, patient one we'd seen up to now. "Well, gentlemen, if you think you've seen some beautiful jewels up to now, get ready to be even more dazzled. Naomi has arrived."

5.
Love at First Sight

I do not consider myself a romantic type. Not at all. But if you've ever dreamed of romance, the girl in your mind has to be beyond gorgeous, right?

Okay, now imagine that girl walking through the door—the real thing. Perfect in every way. So perfect that there's no possible way she would ever look at you twice.

Now you have some idea how I felt when the real Naomi Dowd walked into her dressing room, where the rest of us were waiting for her. Joe will tell you that it doesn't take much in the way of feminine beauty to strike me speechless. I've been turned into jelly so many times it's not funny. It's almost like a tic with me, or a stutter. I can't help it, I have *zero* cool in situations like that.

But trust me, this was on a whole other level.

I can't even tell you what she was wearing—I don't remember, except I do know she looked incredible in it. Her long blond hair was tied back in a ponytail—I guessed some expensive hairdresser would be doing it up for that night's show—and she looked around at us with a big, bright smile. "Hi, everybody!" she said in a breathy voice. "Some place this is, huh?"

None of us answered at first. Then Carrera said, "Great to see you, Naomi darling." Going up to her, he gave her an air kiss on one cheek, then on the other. "You're looking lovely, as always."

"Oh, Vincent," she said, "you're such a flatterer."

From this, I figured out that they knew each other. Of course they did—why wouldn't they? He was a promoter—the one who'd arranged for her to be in this show. They seemed friendly enough, but I didn't sense any romantic attachment between them. Somehow, that made me feel good, like maybe she was "available."

You know, just in case.

"Let me introduce you to everyone, Naomi darling," Carrera went on. Taking her by the arm, he led her farther into the room—which was really big for a dressing room, if you ask me. It had two large sinks, a long mirror surrounded by bright lightbulbs, three really comfortable chairs, drawers, counter-tops, shelves, and a big closet.

"This is Mr. Harris, head of security," Carrera said.

"Pleasure to meet you," Naomi said, offering him her hand.

Harris took it but didn't seem sure whether to shake it or kiss it. "Hal. Please," he said, just holding it.

"Okay—Hal, then," Naomi said, beaming a smile at him. Then she looked over at Joe and me.

"And these are the Hardy brothers," Carrera said. "Frank and Joe."

"Um, Joe and Frank," Joe corrected him.

Naomi giggled and looked us over with a twinkle in her eyes. "And what are you here for?" she asked. "Are you modeling too?"

Whoa—she thought we were good looking enough to be models? Or wait—maybe she was just joking.

I was so nervous, it was hard to tell.

"The Hardys are acting as personal security for you and Shakira," Carrera explained. "They'll be undercover."

The mention of the name Shakira brought the first frown to Naomi's face. "I see," she said, a frosty edge to her voice. "Well, which one of you is mine?"

I froze solid. What I meant to say was, "ME!!!" But I knew Joe was probably thinking the same thing. I didn't want to make a jerk out of myself, so I kept quiet and let him answer. What he said totally surprised me.

"Well, I guess we ought to leave that up to you, Ms. Dowd."

"My, my, my," she said, grinning and letting out a little giggle. "Hmmm. Let me see. . . ." She walked up to Joe and felt his bicep. "You must work out a lot," she said.

"Um, yeah, I guess I do," Joe said. I had to smile—Joe's usually so smooth with girls, but with Naomi, he was acting more like me.

Then she walked over to me and looked me right in the eye. I tried to hold her gaze but wound up looking down at my shoes.

"So you're Frank?"

"Mm-hmm."

"You're cute," she said, running a finger over my cheek.

I know I must have gone beet red, because Naomi chuckled softly. "You think you can keep me safe for one night?"

I nodded. I couldn't even get it together to say yes.

"Well, I can't choose between you," she said. "You both seem fine to me."

"Thanks," Joe said. "You're pretty fine yourself."

I cringed. He sounded like such a jerk, I felt sorry for him.

"Well, I think we can let you three work it out for yourselves," Carrera said, rubbing his manicured hands together. "We'd better be getting on, then, Mr. Harris, Chief Collig. Lots to do before tonight. You boys can stay here for now. I'll let you know when Shakira arrives."

They left, and now it was just me, Naomi, and Joe.

"So, Frank," Joe said.

"So, Joe," I replied.

I could tell that neither of us was going to give an inch.

"We could shoot for it," he said. "Odds or evens?"

"Odds," I said. "One, two, three, shoot!"

I put out two fingers, and Joe put out one. *Yes!*

"Two out of three," he said.

"No way."

"Yes, way."

"Hey, bro—age before beauty, right?" I said.

Naomi turned back to Joe. "You don't mind, do you?"

"Uh . . . no!" Joe said, lying through his teeth. "Hey, fair's fair."

"It'll all work out," she said. "And I've got a really good feeling about Joe here."

"Frank," I corrected her.

She giggled and put a hand to her mouth. "Oops! Sorry."

"It's okay. Don't worry about it," I said.

"Sorry, Joe," she said. "I hope you're not too disappointed. After all, you get to guard Shakira, and she's not exactly hideous, even if she is a total brat."

That caught my attention. So Naomi and Shakira had some bad blood between them. . . . I wondered if Shakira really was a brat, or if Naomi just had a beef with her. In my experience, it usually takes two to tango. Or to have a fight, for that matter.

"In fact, most guys think she's pretty fly," Naomi finished.

"Yeah. I guess so." Joe smiled, but his heart wasn't in it.

Just the day before, he'd been saying how he thought Shakira was even better looking than Naomi. But now, after meeting Naomi face-to-face, I'm sure he was totally incapable of thinking about any other girl in the universe.

"Well," he said, "I guess I'll . . . take a walk around . . . scout things out for tonight." He gave me a look that was pure envy. "Have fun," he said, and walked out of the room, leaving the door open behind him.

"So," Naomi said, turning back to me. She took her bag off her shoulder and plopped it down on the makeup counter. "What do you guys do in this town—when you're not on the job, that is?"

"Um, well, we—" I was about to say we were secret agents for ATAC. That's how hypnotized I was by her. But I caught myself just in time. "We're amateur detectives."

"That's pretty cool," Naomi said, biting her lip in a way that made her even more beautiful. "I'd love to do that—except, of course, I never have time for anything that's fun. It's the same old thing every day—shows, shoots, and parties, shows, shoots, and parties, all day and all night." She let out a sigh. "So tiring."

"It sounds like fun to me," I said.

"Try doing it for a couple months straight, and then see how much fun it is," she said. "Don't get me wrong—I'm not complaining or anything. But it's not as glamorous as it looks. Not by a long shot."

"I imagine there's a lot of money in it," I said.

"Oh, yeah, but you know . . . it goes. The lifestyle's molto expensivo."

"I guess so." I was starting to feel uncomfortable, alone in this little room with her. I knew she was just a human being, like everyone else—but somehow, to me, she wasn't.

"You think Frank will be okay?" she asked.

"Oh, yeah. Don't worry about *Joe*." I added a little emphasis to Joe's name this time.

"Oops! Sorry again. I'm terrible with names."

"It's okay. Joe's a big boy—even though I'm the older brother," I added, just in case she thought I was too young for her. "He can take care of himself."

"I'm curious," she said, suddenly serious. "Why did they think Shakira and I needed extra security?"

"I think they're worried about the jewelry being stolen. You know, with it being so expensive and all. And there's that, um, warlord guy, Sanguillen. The guy who had the jewels confiscated? I hear they lost track of him last week." I was giving a lot of information—but it wasn't information I thought needed to be kept secret.

"Oh! I see." She thought about that for a minute, taking it in. "I heard he did some awful things to people over there in Australia."

"The Philippines, actually. Yeah. So . . ."

"But they don't need to worry about *me*," she said. "I mean, after all, I've already got Bobo."

"Bobo?"

"Somebody call me?" a loud, gravelly voice barked from over my left shoulder. I looked up—and there, standing in the doorway, and taking up every last inch of it, was the most menacing hulk of concrete I'd seen in a long time.

"Oh, Bobo—there you are!" Naomi said. "Come on in and meet Joe—Joe, this is Bobo Hines. My full-time bodyguard."

I got up and stuck out my hand. "It's Frank, actually. Pleased to meet you, Bobo."

Bobo walked slowly toward me, sizing me up—probably trying to figure out how hard he'd have to blow on me to knock me unconscious. Finally he took my hand, and squeezed so hard he nearly crushed every bone in it. "Good to meet you, Frank," he said, staring right through me.

"Don't get the wrong idea," Naomi said, "Bobo's a sweetheart. He wouldn't hurt a fly—unless, of course, that naughty fly was threatening me. Right, Bobo?"

Bobo didn't smile, or even twitch. Still staring at me, he said, "Word. So . . . what's *he* doing here?"

Meaning *me*.

"Oh, Frank's been assigned to guard me until the show's over," she explained. "Isn't he cute? I think he's so cute!"

"Yeah," said Bobo, gripping my hand even harder. "Real cute."

"Uh, could I have my hand back now, please?" I gasped, red flashes shooting across my vision from the pain.

He released my hand, which was somewhere between numb and throbbing. "Yeah. Sure thing." Then he turned to her. "What do you need a bodyguard for? You have me."

"It wasn't my idea, Bobo," she said. "Go talk to the police if you don't like it."

He winced at the mention of the police.

Bobo was wearing cargo shorts with no belt, no socks, and old sneakers with the laces untied. His shirt had no sleeves—well, to be perfectly exact, they'd been ripped off at the shoulders, exposing his huge, rocklike muscles, covered all over with tattoos.

There were snakes, and scorpions, and skulls, and the letters RIP, and numbers, and Asian characters—this guy was a walking sideshow. And I, for one, also had no idea why *anyone* thought they needed *me* to help *him* guard Naomi.

Unless, of course, they didn't *trust* Bobo. Which I could totally understand. I could easily see a guy like him working for the mob, or for some bloodthirsty warlord, for that matter.

I was just thinking that maybe I'd made a mistake and should have let Joe take the job of guarding Naomi, when she said, "Bobo, did you see my iPod? I think I left it in the limo."

"Nope," he said, not taking his eyes off me.

"Could you go and check?"

He didn't seem wild about the idea. "Why can't Wimpy here go check?" he said.

"Don't be silly, Bobo. Frank"—she smiled (she knew my name!)—"doesn't even know where the limo is. We'll be right here waiting for you, don't worry."

"I don't know. . . ." he said, flexing his scary muscles and balling his hands into fists.

"You can totally trust Frank," she assured him. "I already do." She gave me a smile that would have melted me into jelly if Bobo hadn't been standing there.

"Okay," he grunted. "Whatever." Sticking his finger in my face, he said, "Behave yourself, understand?"

"Totally," I said—squeaked, actually.

"I'll be right back."

He left us there, and I exhaled for the first time since he'd grabbed my hand.

Naomi giggled. "Bobo's really a pussycat," she said. "He's just very devoted to me, that's all."

"Yeah," I said. "A real pussycat." I shook my hand out, trying to regain the feeling in it.

"Are you okay, Frank?"

"Fine," I said. "I've got another hand, anyway."

That giggle again. "You're sweet," she said. Reaching for my good hand, the left one, she drew me over to her and gave me a kiss on the cheek. "Cute, too. I'm glad you're here. I feel safer with you around."

"Really?" I said. "Seems like Bobo could take care of anything that came up."

She shook her head. "He's not too bright," she said in a half whisper. "He never finished third grade, you know?"

"Aha. What's he been up to since then?"

She sighed. "He's had a rough life," she said, but didn't go into any more detail. "But he's turned the corner now."

"Glad to hear it."

"Frank?" She got up, came over to me, and put her arms around my neck. "Can I tell you a secret?"

I could barely breathe. Her face was only inches from mine, and I thought I might even faint. "Um . . . sure . . ."

"I'm scared about tonight."

"You are?"

"Uh-huh."

"Why?"

"When you said the mob might try something? Well, that got me thinking . . . you know, Shakira used to have a boyfriend in the mob."

"She did?"

This was news to me—and not good news either. "Who was it?"

"I forget his name, but it was a weird one . . . something about shivering . . ." She wrinkled her perfect brow, trying to remember it. "But I remember he did time in Sing Sing, for jewelry theft."

Alarm bells were going off in my head. Really loud ones. "His name wasn't Shakey, was it?" I asked.

"Yeah, that's it—Shakey. Shakey Twist! How did you know?"

6.

Something Wicked This Way Comes

I prowled around the inner corridors of the convention center for about an hour, stopping a few times in the control room, which was now fully occupied. I asked the operators how long they'd been there, and they told me they'd been at their posts since before the diamonds had arrived.

I checked their names against the roster posted on Harris's computer, and they all checked out. So these people had all gone through security clearances before even being hired. I felt that I could trust at least this part of the convention center's security. If the mob had a plan to steal the diamonds and had someone on the inside, at least it wasn't in the control room.

I was still worried about those air shafts, to be

honest. I wondered if the mob, or Sanguillen, could have placed people inside them before security even showed up. But I dismissed that possibility. How would anyone survive that long in an air shaft without food or water—or, come to think of it, a bathroom?

I wandered outside and did a circuit of the entire convention center. I saw security teams checking cameras mounted on trucks, testing alarm systems, and patrolling the perimeter of the complex.

No shortage of people on duty, at least. In fact, if anything, there were too many of them to be efficient. The logos on the security trucks were from three different companies!

I was on a grassy hill overlooking the main gate when I saw a stretch limo pull up, surrounded front and back by Bayport Police cruisers. The police deployed on all sides of the limo as the chauffeur went around to open the passenger door.

And out stepped Shakira.

Oh, man! She was wearing a white fur coat, which she immediately slipped out of and handed to the chauffeur. "Leave it in the limo," she told him. Without even looking his way, she sashayed past him and through the open gate.

I bounded down the hill after her, eager to introduce myself before she went inside.

Bayport's finest stopped me. "Hey, it's Joe Hardy!" said Lieutenant Rogers, a friend of ours on the force. "Whatcha doin' here, Joe?"

"Haven't you heard?" I answered, brushing the wrinkles out of my shirt. "I've been hired to look after Ms. Shakira here. Just for today."

"Get out!" he said with a laugh. "Nice try, Joe. Shoulda thoughta that one myself."

"No, it's true!" I insisted. "Ask Mr. Harris."

"The head of security? Okay, let's do that." He whipped out his walkie-talkie and called in his ID.

Meanwhile, Shakira had been taking all this in. She gave me a big smile and a wink, and I could tell right away I'd made the right decision letting Frank guard Naomi.

"Harris says you're legit," Lieutenant Rogers said, sticking his walkie-talkie back in its belt holster. "Congratulations, Joe—I don't know how you managed to get the job, but any time you need some help . . ."

"Sure thing," I said, clapping him on the back. "I'll take it from here, guys." I offered Shakira my arm. "May I show you inside?"

She slipped her arm through mine and gazed at me with a twinkle in her huge, brown eyes. "Nice going . . . Joe. I think this is the start of a beautiful friendship."

And if I wasn't hooked before—well, now I was toast.

"Let me take you down to your dressing room, Ms. Shakira."

"Oh, come on, Joe—it's just Shakira, okay?"

"Sure. Sh-Shakira."

We walked arm in arm down the hallway, with me pulling her huge rolling suitcase.

"So, a personal bodyguard?" she said with a sly grin. "How did I rate getting one of those?"

"I, uh, I think they just want to make sure you're okay—I mean, the jewelry's worth a lot of money, and, well, y'know . . ."

"They're afraid someone's gonna take it, aren't they?" she said, letting out a scornful laugh. "Well, you know, Joe, if someone really wants to take it, nobody can stop them."

"Well, I'll sure try," I assured her.

Again, that laugh. "You're a nice boy, Joe," she said. "I like you. But trust me, if somebody wants that jewelry badly enough—and by somebody, I mean somebody *big*—not you, not the police, not Superman or Batman or Spiderman or any man is man enough to prevent it."

I took that as a personal challenge—with a secret bonus. If someone tried to steal the jewels, and I stopped them, Shakira would rate me as a superhero.

We reached the dressing-room area and passed right by the open door of Naomi's room. Shakira stopped in her tracks. "Well, well, well," she said, seeing Naomi and Frank sitting close to one another. "Look what the cat dragged in."

Naomi shook her head and frowned. "This could have been such a classy show, and they had to go and ruin it by inviting you."

"What happened to your ex-con bodyguard?" Shakira asked. "What was his name, Dodo?"

"Bobo," Naomi spat back. "He went to get my iPod. This is Frank. Frank Hardy. He's my bodyguard for the day." She saw me and waved. "Hello, Joe. I see you found her. I hope you don't feel too bad about having to guard her."

"Frank's my brother," I explained to Shakira. "And I don't feel bad about guarding you. Not at all."

"Of course you don't," she said, stroking my cheek with her long, painted nails. "She just thinks she's all that and a bag of chips. Even though her bodyguard has spent more time in Sing Sing than out."

"Speaking of ex-cons," Naomi said, "how's your boyfriend Shakey?"

Shakira, who had been about to move on,

stopped. "You know I haven't even seen him in three months," she said. "At least I dated a top dog. You're the one who associates with the dregs."

"Bobo's loyal, at least," Naomi shot back. "And he cares about me—even though we're just friends, and always will be."

"Come on, Joe," Shakira said, grabbing my sleeve and pulling me on down the hall, "I can't take any more of her jive."

Her dressing room was just a few doors down. It was exactly like Naomi's, in reverse—kind of like their personalities, in fact.

I'll be honest—I was already in love. Not only was she fine in the extreme, she also had the brass to sling it out with the likes of Naomi Dowd, who'd had me tongue-tied just an hour before.

"I don't want you getting any wrong ideas," Shakira said. She shut the door of the dressing room, opened her suitcase, and immediately started hanging up her clothes for the show—a series of incredible outfits ranging from gowns to, well . . . I guess they were bathing suits.

"I went out with this guy, Shakey," she said, coming right out with it. "He used to be a real bad dude—been in Sing Sing for something, I forget what—oh, yeah, jaywalking! Can you imagine going to prison for jaywalking? There was some tax cheating, too, I think—but that was a long time ago. For two years he's been out of that place, and while I was seeing him, he was legit, just like you or me."

SUSPECT PROFILE

<u>Name:</u> Bobo Hines

<u>Hometown:</u> Brooklyn, NY

<u>Physical description:</u> Age 25, 6', 3", 246 lbs. of solid rock muscle. Pockmarked, mealy complexion, shaved head, beady black eyes that always look suspicious and angry. So many tattoos he could open up a store. Bad teeth, bad breath, bad dude.

<u>Occupation:</u> Personal security guard/bodyguard for Naomi Dowd. Could be something more, but no one really knows.

<u>Background:</u> Abandoned as a baby in a garbage can in Brooklyn, Bobo came up the hard way. Third-grade dropout, and never known for his brains. The Downtown Huggermuggers gang became his family when he was nine. Got his first tattoo at eleven, served his first time at thirteen, in juvie. Graduated to Sing-Sing for armed robbery and assault with a deadly weapon (his fists). There he met lots of guys even meaner than him—including the notorious

mobster Shakey Twist. Bobo claims to have gone straight since his release—and he does have a good job with Naomi, though no one knows what made her hire him. Was she really just trying to polish her image?

<u>Suspicious behavior:</u> It's more his past than his present that's worrying-but he's mean and dangerous, the kind of guy who could blow at any moment.

<u>Suspected of:</u> Being the inside man in Shakey Twist's plot to steal the diamonds from the convention center. Who better than him? They know each other from Sing-Sing, right?

<u>Possible motive:</u> Naomi pays well—but not that well.

"Meanwhile, her precious Bobo probably got out last week—with a new tattoo, I'll bet. What was he in for this time? Assault? Armed robbery?"

"He was in prison?"

"Oh, yeah—didn't she tell you?"

"I, uh, really didn't get a chance to talk to her much."

"Tell me something about the great Miss Naomi Dowd—if she's so prim and proper, never been in trouble or anything, how come she picks a guy like that to be her bodyguard?"

"I, um, couldn't really say. . . ."

"I haven't even *got* a bodyguard!" Shakira went on, basically forgetting I was even there. She was pacing the room half the time, and spent the other half hanging up her outfits. "I don't *need* a bodyguard—just let someone try and mess with me! I'm tough. Raised on the streets of Brooklyn."

"Really? Brooklyn, huh?"

"That's right, Dwight."

"Joe. Joe Hardy."

She stopped, caught herself, and laughed shyly. "Sorry—I know it's Joe. Dwight, that's just an expression. As in, "Hop on the bus, Gus. Make a new plan, Stan.""

"Watch your head, Fred."

"Ha! You're funny!" She took my hand in hers. "What do you know, Joe?" She nodded slowly, looking at me the whole time. "Listen, you don't think I'm part of any 'inside thing,' do you?"

"Huh?"

"Inside thing. You know—because I went out with someone in the mob. And there are all these jewels. . . ."

"If the people putting this show together had

58

thought that, they wouldn't have asked you to model," I said.

"Maybe they had second thoughts," she said sadly, still looking at me. "Maybe that's why they hired you—to keep an eye on me. Make sure I don't do anything bad."

"Nah. I mean, they hired my brother to watch Naomi, right?"

She seemed to consider this for a second. "I guess you're right—but let me tell you something about Naomi. Her career is this"—she held her thumb and forefinger a teeny bit apart—"close to over, and when it is, guess who's gonna be the next big thing?"

"You?"

"That's right, Joe. You're looking at her. I'm just biding my time, that's all. Biding my time. She's got a big fall coming, that Naomi. And when she falls, nobody's gonna pick her up, because she's been mean to every one of them."

Her anger shook me, and for the first time, I took a step back and considered Shakira from a distance. Obviously, she hated Naomi with a passion. But why? Was it just professional rivalry? Or was there something more . . . something deeper, and more dangerous?

SUSPECT PROFILE

Name: Shakira

Hometown: Ocean Point, New Jersey

Physical description: Age 20, 5', 9", weight... well, skinny. Mocha complexion, long, shiny, reddish-brown hair, huge dark eyes, full lips.

Occupation: Up-and-coming supermodel, probably number two in the world right now in earnings per year, behind only Naomi Dowd.

Background: Born and raised in Brooklyn, discovered when she won an international teen modeling contest and was signed by the biggest agency in America. Unmarried. No present boyfriend, but has had several in the past— among them the notorious gangster from Atlantic City, Shakey Twist.

Suspicious behavior: Moody, and she's got a real temper. Also, seems to have it in for Naomi Dowd, or is it the other way around—or both?

Suspected of: Being part of Shakey Twist's plot to steal the diamonds from the convention center. She says she and Shakey are a thing of the past, but is she telling the truth?

Possible motive: Are you kidding? Diamonds are forever!

"I think I'm going to lie down and rest for a while," she said. "It's been a long flight. I was on the red-eye from Antwerp."

"Antwerp?" That was where Carlos Sanguillen had gone missing!

She yawned and stretched. "Would you mind waiting outside for me? I promise I won't steal anything in the meantime."

She smiled so I'd know she was joking. But you know what they say—there really are no jokes. On some level, she wanted me out of her sight.

I felt hurt, rejected. If she didn't want me around while she slept, it was because I hadn't earned her trust—yet. "Sure. I'll sit just outside the door, okay?"

"So long as it's shut tight," she said, yawning again—a little too much of a yawn to be real, I thought.

Something wasn't smelling right here.

"Here's my cell number, in case you need to reach me." She handed me her business card. It had her face on it. I put it in my pocket as a souvenir. Whether or not I ever called that number, I was going to keep her card for life.

I shut the door behind me and sat down on a stool I'd brought out into the hall with me. Behind the door, I heard the shower going—and then I heard Shakira speaking. She was talking on her cell phone, I realized. But she'd turned on the shower so I wouldn't hear what she was saying.

With time to kill, I sat there, thinking. I asked myself, if I were planning a big jewel heist in this place, how would I do it?

First I'd have to disable the perimeter protection systems—the closed-circuit cameras and the motion-sensing laser-based alarm systems. To shut down the motion detectors, I'd just have to pay a secret visit to the circuit-breaker boxes. For the cameras, I'd either have to shut off all the power to the entire convention center—and they'd have a backup system in place—or I'd have to get to every one of those cameras and disable them individually.

No, wait—I wouldn't have to get to *all* of them. Just the ones that covered the area I was going to pass through on my way in and out of the center.

If I wasn't already inside.

I stared up at the air vents embedded in the ceiling of the hall. Someone could get through to the hall where the diamonds were by shimmying through the ducts. Of course, they'd have to get past the police guarding all the entrances—unless they removed a grate and climbed in through it.

But back to the cameras. They'd still have to disable them. . . .

And then I thought back to the moment before Shakira's arrival had distracted me. I'd been thinking there were too many different security firms working on this job. Three of them, in fact. . . .

I knew I was right. There was something fishy going on, but I'd let myself get distracted. I wanted to hop right off my chair and go running back outside to get the names of the three firms and the license plate numbers on their trucks. I wanted to alert the police and Mr. Harris that there was something wrong—but my job was to stay with Shakira.

I walked slowly down the hallway. "Frank?" I called out in a soft voice.

"Yeah?" He popped his head out through Naomi's open doorway.

"I think something's fishy outside—with the camera setups and the breaker boxes. I want to go check, but . . ." I nodded toward Shakira's closed dressing-room door. "Do you think you could cover for me? Just for a few minutes?"

"I don't know," he said. "Her bodyguard, Bobo? He should have been back by now, but he isn't. He went to get her iPod from the limo."

"I'm sure he'll be back any minute, bro," I said. "He can look out for Naomi while you watch Shakira till I get back."

"I'm sure he'll be happy to," Frank said, making a face.

"Cool. Stay alert, bro," I said as I took off down the hallway. "I think something's up, and it isn't good."

I jogged around the corner and down the adjoining hallway until I got to the diamond room. The door was closed, of course, and the only way to get in would have been to press my ID'd palm against the ceramic panel—but I didn't, because I heard voices inside. Men's voices.

I couldn't tell who they belonged to, and I didn't have long to figure it out—because just then, a strong, muscular arm wrapped itself around my throat, and a hand holding a wet hankie pressed itself over my mouth and nose.

I smelled chloroform, saw stars—and everything spun into blackness.

7.

From the Frying Pan into the Fire

"I can't imagine where Bobo could have gone to," Naomi was saying. "I mean, how hard is it to find a rainbow-painted stretch limo?" She was sitting at her makeup mirror, playing with some eyeliner—but really, she seemed more interested in talking to *me*.

If only I didn't feel so nervous around her, I might have held up my end of the conversation better. Whenever she started asking me questions about my life, I was reduced to one-word answers like "Yeah," or "I guess." (Okay, that's two words—sorry.)

Within half an hour, I knew the following: She was twenty years old, born in Indiana and raised in Chicago, where she was spotted in a modeling contest at age eight. By the age of sixteen, she was the world's most famous runway model and cover girl. For the past four years, it had been impossible to avoid seeing her face—on a billboard, a magazine, a TV commercial, a music video—you get the idea.

Yet alone with her, here in the dressing room, she seemed like just an ordinary girl—except, of course, she wasn't. Not anymore. I was getting to see the real Naomi—the Naomi she kept inside except for rare moments like this, when she got to spend an hour with someone who wasn't "in the business" or trying to get next to her for selfish reasons.

I was there to protect her, that was all. To make sure she didn't get hurt if somebody tried to steal these incredible diamonds. And for that, she appreciated me. Liked me, even.

How lucky was I?

Of course, I knew I was supposed to be keeping an eye on Shakira while Joe was off checking out the cameras and circuit-breaker boxes. And I did take a quick look down the hallway every two minutes or so. But my first job was to keep an eye on Naomi, after all.

"I hope he's okay," she said, biting her lip.

"Who?"

"Bobo, silly. Hello, Earth to Frank?"

"Sorry. I was just thinking."

"You think a lot, don't you?"

"Me? Yeah, I guess."

See what I mean? I wasn't exactly impressing her with my witty conversation.

"He never leaves me alone for very long," she said, her perfect brows knitting with worry. "There must be some problem."

"I think Bobo can take care of himself," I said.

She laughed. "He *is* pretty strong. One time, this guy got out of hand with me at a party—and Bobo, you should have seen him, he had that guy in a headlock in two seconds flat. I'll bet his head still hurts, Bobo squeezed it so hard!"

"I'll bet."

"He's very devoted to me, you know," she said with a sweet smile. "I mean, I hired him at a very good salary, at a time when he couldn't get a job."

"How'd you meet him?" I asked.

"Oh, I was doing a show in Atlantic City, and the crowds were really over the top. Vincent—he promoted that show too—thought I needed protection, so he talked with some people down there, and the next day, Bobo showed up. I realized I'd seen him the day before under the boardwalk, hanging out with a bunch of guys who looked like gangsters. But once Vincent put him in a suit, he looked fine."

"Uh huh. So, let me get this straight—Vincent finds this guy on the street, doesn't know him from Adam, and hires him to protect you?"

She blinked a few times, looking confused. "Yeah, I guess that does sound strange—but I mean, look at Bobo. Would you bother me if you saw him standing next to me, protecting me?"

"I guess not," I had to admit.

"So anyway, I decided to hire Bobo for my protection wherever I went. Still, I'm glad you're here, Frank." She reached out and took my hand. Her eyes locked onto mine. "You're smart—much smarter than Bobo, not that that's such a great achievement. And I'm going to need somebody smart to protect me once those jewels are around my neck." She drew me closer to her. "You . . . will protect me, won't you?"

"Count on it," I whispered, unable to find my voice.

She leaned in and kissed me on the cheek. "Good," she said. "I feel much safer now."

I heard a hostile grunt behind me and turned to see Bobo's hulking figure blocking the doorway. Had he been there the whole time? While Naomi was kissing me, and telling me how much smarter than him I was?

I sure hoped not.

"I don't like him being here," he said to Naomi, never taking his eyes off me. "I don't trust this guy."

"He's fine, Bobo," Naomi said, clucking her tongue. "Stop being so suspicious."

"I got my eye on you, babyface," he said to me. "Don't try nothing."

Mmm-hmm. Not the brightest bulb in the pack.

"Listen, I'd better check in with Shakira," I said. "Joe asked me to keep an eye on her while he was gone . . . and he's been gone quite a while now."

All this time I'd been trying to get around Bobo and out the door of the dressing room. But he wasn't letting me through.

"Listen, you," he said, grabbing me by the shirt and bringing my face right up to his. "You lay one finger on her, and you're a dead man, understand?"

"Hey, big guy," I said, trying to laugh it off but failing, "I'm on her side too. We're all on the same team, okay?"

He let go of my shirt. "Remember what I said," he growled, then let me pass.

"Naomi, I'll . . . be back in a few minutes, okay?"

"I'll be right here," she said, blowing me a kiss.

Bobo saw *that*. He gave me a look that would

have burned right through me if I'd stayed there one more second.

I was going to have to stay on the big guy's good side if I expected to do my job of keeping close to Naomi—but how was I supposed to stay on his good side?

I couldn't help thinking he was the wrong guy to be protecting her day in and day out. She needed someone much more presentable. More intelligent. Someone like . . . me, for instance.

I knocked on Shakira's dressing room door. "Um, hi there. Is Joe back yet?"

She was alone, sitting there looking sad and fragile and incredibly beautiful. I couldn't believe Joe would just leave her there alone for so long!

"He abandoned me here," she said. "Nice, huh? So you're his brother?"

"Frank," I reminded her, and we shook hands.

"Sit down, Frank," she said. "Are you in security too?"

"Uh, yeah," I said. "I'm assigned to Naomi for today."

"Oh," she said, taken aback. "Well, what are you doing here, then? Spying on me for her?" She was joking, but I could tell she half meant it.

"Me? No, no. Joe asked me to keep an eye on you while he was gone—and Naomi's already got her bodyguard, so I thought I'd see how you were getting along."

"I'm fine," she said. "Really. You know, the whole bodyguard thing can get out of hand. I used to have a whole gang of them trailing me around—I think they caused more problems than they solved, starting fights and stuff like that. And like I told your brother, I'm used to looking out for myself. Been doing it since I was a little girl."

"Well, I'm glad you're okay," I said. "But once you start putting on the jewelry, we're going to have to stick close by the two of you. Just in case."

She sighed. "Those diamonds are bad news," she said. "Bad karma, as they say. People were killed and their families destroyed to collect them. Now they want to sell them for charity. Well, that's all good, but I still say the whole thing is creepy."

I nodded. "I'm afraid creepy may be the least of it."

There was a short, rapid knock on the door. "Shakira, darling, it's Vincent. We need you onstage for a walk-through."

"Already?" Shakira moaned. "All right, I'm coming." She opened the door, and I followed her out into the hallway.

"Oh. Hello there," Vincent Carrera said. He seemed unpleasantly surprised to see me. "I thought your friend was guarding Shakira."

"My brother. He is."

"Ah. Well, he won't be needed for an hour or so. We're doing a rehearsal with Naomi and Shakira."

"But our job is to stay with them," I said.

"Well, you can stay with them after," Carrera insisted. "We've got a job to do. There'll be plenty of us around to keep an eye on the girls." He gave me a weak smile, and I found myself gritting my teeth and balling up my fists.

But I let them go. Part of me was worried about Joe, anyway, and I wanted to see where he'd gone off to.

I went down the hallway Joe had taken. I passed a few security personnel guarding the exhibit hall where the diamonds were stored, and some more on the stairs leading up to the main level.

But no sign of Joe. On the main level I found an exit door and went outside for some fresh air. It was five thirty, two hours to showtime.

The sun was glowing over the bay—a fantastic sight. Turning inland, I could see a line of cars and limos snaking up to the convention center's main entrance and valet parking area. The guests were arriving for the big show. Most were dressed to the nines. Clearly, this was the place to see and be seen tonight. Flashes popped as paparazzi surrounded each new arrival.

Joe's absence was really starting to bother me. He wouldn't have just left Shakira alone for that long unless he was chasing down a lead—or a criminal. . . . He'd said there was something fishy about the camera trucks . . . or was it the breaker boxes . . . or both?

I decided to circle the outside of the convention center, checking each camera position and breaker box along the way—starting in the rear, away from the crowds. If there was any funny business going on, it would have to be done away from the focus of attention.

A few times Bayport police stopped me—they don't *all* know me—and I had to show them my security clearance. I realized that any thieves posing as maintenance crews would have to have passes like mine to get through the police lines. But if the mob was planning to hit a target this big, they'd have gotten themselves passes somehow. Hey, *I* had one, didn't I?

I saw three different security firms' trucks parked around the outside of the center. I thought it was a little odd, but then, if you wanted to be extra secure, you'd have different firms keeping an eye on each other, right?

I was halfway around now, and so far, everything looked normal. On this side, there was a chain-link fence to my left, walling off a construction zone—the convention center was so new, they were still adding on to it.

As I passed, I noticed that the chain links had been cut and then repaired. Could someone have slipped through and then tried to cover their tracks?

I was passing one of the utility entrances when I noticed something different. Here there was just one truck. It belonged to the only firm of the three that wasn't locally based and known to me: Hanley Security, New York, NY.

I figured Vincent had to have hired this firm from the big city. He was the kind of guy who didn't trust rubes like us, even if we did have the newest, hottest convention center in the East.

What interested me, though, was that the truck was empty, but running. Where were its driver and crew?

Two cables led from the rear of the truck toward the convention center. I followed them along the ground. They disappeared inside a slightly opened set of utility doors.

If I were Joe and I'd seen that, I'd definitely have gone inside to see what was up.

I peeked through the open doorway and saw that the cable led to a transformer box. Three men wearing Hanley Security jackets were huddled around it. I followed the wire up the wall from the trans-former—to a box marked MASTER ALARM CIRCUITS.

They looked up and saw me . . . and I saw them—three faces that could have been the models for any murderer's mug shot.

I can still see those horrible, scarred faces, even though I never laid eyes on them again. They were the last thing I saw before the chloroformed hankie was jammed under my nose, and I passed out cold.

8.

Zero Hour

I woke up with a headache that felt like a spike going from ear to ear, right through my skull.

I couldn't see a thing. For a minute I thought I'd been blinded—but then I saw that it wasn't completely dark. There were the outlines of objects, flickering in the light of a computer monitor. The monitor was just playing its "sleep" pattern of stars in the night sky that seem to be coming right at you. You know the one.

It was probably good that the room was so dark, because I was pretty sure any bright light would have jiggled that spike between my ears.

I tried to get up but couldn't. My feet were tied together, and my hands were bound behind my back, fastened to some sack of cement, or sand, or something. . . .

Something that was *breathing*!

Snoring, in fact. Come to think of it, I knew that snore. I'd have known it anywhere, spike in my head or no.

"Frank!" I whispered. "Frank! Wake up, man!"

Nothing. Frank was out cold, probably on the same chloroform cocktail—I was pretty sure that's what it was—that had knocked me for a loop. He would have been at least fifteen minutes behind me—it would have taken him that long to get suspicious and/or worried about me.

So I figured it'd be a while before he woke up. Meantime, I continued to survey the room, while I tried to go over in my mind how I could get us out of this mess.

Let's see . . . I had an all-purpose knife thingy in the back pocket of my cargo pants. . . .

Too bad I couldn't reach it.

I saw a pair of scissors on a desk across the room, but that would have to wait until Frank woke up.

My eyes were adjusting now, and I could see that we were in some sort of guard kiosk—maybe an unused entrance to the parking garage, judging by the sounds of engines on the other side of the wall.

77

But if it was a guard post, where was the guard?

I looked around, and saw another sack of cement lying behind the desk, with its feet sticking out—bound together, of course.

Okay, so much for the guard. This all added up to one thing—a heist was already in progress. The diamond show was about to start, if it hadn't already. And Frank and I, whose job it was to protect Naomi and Shakira, were tied together—totally useless!

"Frank!"

"Whagumphr?"

"Frank, wake up, man! We're missing everything!"

"Hmmzt?"

"The show! *Frank!*"

"Okay, okay, I'm okay, yeah, okay . . . Okay."

He didn't seem okay—but at least he was awake.

"Notice anything, bro?" I asked.

"Ow, my head!"

"Chloroform, dude. You and me both."

"My hands . . ."

"Exactly. Do you think you could get it together enough to reach into my back pocket and pull out my knife thingy?

"This is pretty humiliating," I muttered as he tried to find it. "Did you have to go and get yourself jumped?"

"Hey, I was just trying to find *you*, bro," he said, coming to.

"Oh, right, this is all *my* fault."

"Well, if the shoe fits . . ."

"Shut up and cut me loose, okay?" I said, really getting annoyed—although it was *me* I really could have kicked. How could I have let myself get ambushed like a total amateur? "Hey—watch it," I said. "That's my wrist you're cutting!"

"Sorry," he said. "I'm doing my best. I'm still groggy, y'know?"

"Well, do better!"

"Man, someone woke up on the wrong side of the bed," he said, freeing me at last.

I untied my ankles, rubbed the feeling back into my arms and legs, and stood up.

There were no windows in this control room except for the one next to where the guard was supposed to sit. I went over there and lifted the shade that had been pulled down in front of it—sure enough, it was a parking garage. I didn't see anyone nearby, nor were there any cars. "This must be the end facing the construction zone," I said.

"Perfect place to break in," Frank said, going over to the unconscious guard to check his condition. "He's alive—but I'm sure he didn't have much company, way back here at the far end of the complex."

"Not until the bad guys showed up. Try the door, Frank."

He did. "Locked."

"Figures." I moved my arm, and it hit the computer's mouse. That made the sleep pattern on the monitor go away. Luckily, the guard must have been logged in, because I was able to access the computer's files.

"Call up a schematic of the convention center," Frank said.

"I know what to do," I said, still cranky from my headache.

I called up the schematic, which wasn't hard to find, and it showed a network of passageways, complete with circuits, and those all-important air ducts. Looking up, I spotted one just over my head.

"I'll bet that's how they're getting to the exhibit hall where the diamonds are," Frank said. "Print out a copy of that. Better make it two—one for each of us in case we have to split up."

"Got it," I said, pressing the Print button. The sheets were printed in seconds, and we each whipped out our trusty pocket flashlights, testing them to make sure they were working properly. "Well?" I asked, pointing upward toward the air ducts. "What do you say?"

Frank grabbed a chair and placed it under the grating. "After you."

I unscrewed the grate, then hoisted myself up into the air shaft.

It wasn't that gross, considering. The center was only four months old, so the shafts hadn't had a chance to collect too much dust or mold. Good thing, because Frank is a big sneezer, and we were going to have to keep really quiet up in there. A cool breeze wafted through—also good, because judging from the way it was outdoors, you could have fried an egg in those ducts if the AC wasn't on.

I crawled forward enough to let Frank get up inside. Meanwhile, I checked my schematic drawing. "Okay," I said. "How 'bout we head for the dressing rooms?"

"Shouldn't we go straight to the exhibit hall?"

"Depends whether the diamonds are still there—in other words, whether the show is starting on time."

"Why don't we go by way of the main theater?" Frank suggested. "That way, we'll know where to head next—and it's pretty much on the way to everything from this end of the center."

It was a good plan, and so that's what we did. But let me tell you—it takes time to crawl through an air duct. Lots of time, and we had a long way to go.

The only good part was that, if the thieves were getting in this way too, at least they were no longer gaining on us.

We soon got used to crawling. We had to go slow, though, because we couldn't afford to make any noise—if security or police personnel heard us making a racket up in the air shafts, they might mistake us for thieves. If that happened, they'd shoot first and ask questions later.

We followed our schematic map, and soon, in the distance, we could hear Vincent Carrera's amplified voice. The show was starting!

"Ladies and gentlemen," we heard him say, "welcome to the biggest diamond show of the twenty-first century!"

His voice carried perfectly, echoing down the air duct toward us. It came from everywhere and nowhere, so we still had to use our schematic to guide us, until we arrived at a grate directly over the main theater. Below us sat a crowd of hundreds of people. A lot of the women were wearing gowns and diamonds, with the men mostly in tuxedos. Many of them were looking around to see who else was there.

Scattered among these obviously wealthy folks was a bunch of people equipped with notebooks and charts. I took these to be the professional diamond buyers, probably representing major jewelry firms and stores. They looked like they'd flown in from all over the world. This really was, as Carrera had said, the biggest diamond show of the twenty-first century.

"We are gathered here together for a high purpose, ladies and gentlemen," he was saying. "The fabulous jewels you will be seeing were obtained by illegal means, and captured by the international forces of law and order."

That got a round of applause. When it died down, he continued, "Today we offer them to you, the public—not as illegal gems, but as legally certified jewelry. All proceeds of this show—ALL proceeds, I repeat—will be going to the charities listed in your programs, to help the victims who paid for these gems with their pain and loss. They, and we, are most grateful to you for your generosity. Please bid well, with them in mind."

Funny, but there was a guy sitting in one of the back rows who looked very familiar. I could have sworn he was that Philippine warlord who'd had the diamonds taken from him.

No . . . it couldn't be . . . they wouldn't have let him in here, would they? He'd have been recognized and arrested.

"Hey, Frank," I whispered, "isn't that guy Carlos Sanguillen?"

"Where?"

"Here, I'll move up so you can see—he's sitting two rows from the back, all the way over to the right of the center aisle."

After he'd had a look, Frank said, "That's Carlos Sanguillen, all right—he looks just like his picture."

"Funny he should be here, don't you think?" I asked.

"More than funny. Hey, Joe—he's getting up."

"He is?"

"Yeah, he checked his watch, looked around for something or someone, and now he's leaving the theater out the back door."

SUSPECT PROFILE

<u>Name:</u> Carlos Sanguillen

<u>Hometown:</u> Manila, Philippines

<u>Physical description:</u> Age 40, 5', 9", 140 lbs. Well dressed in dark linen suit and silk tie. Tanned complexion, mean eyes, thick black mustache, longish black hair. Evil-looking guy if there ever was one.

<u>Occupation:</u> Warlord and terrorist. Besides killing, kidnapping, and bombing, makes millions peddling illegally mined diamonds, uses proceeds to buy arms and explosives, etc.

Background: Born and raised in the slums of Manila, moved to Jolo Island as a young man, got involved with gangs there, soon rose to the top by being more violent than any other gangster on the island. Gradually morphed into a guerrilla leader as the army tried to crack down on his operations—but he's still a gangster and killer at heart. Thought to have various wives and girlfriends stashed away, but their identities are a closely guarded secret.

Suspicious behavior: Meetings with Shakey Twist; e-mails that mention Shakey; has been spotted in Antwerp, the international diamond trading center, in the last week; and is now here in Bayport. Just a coincidence? Not likely.

Suspected of: Being Shakey Twist's partner in a plot to steal the diamonds from the convention center.

Possible motive: Millions of dollars' worth of gems returned to their rightful owner, so he can sell them himself, for his own personal charity.

"Something's happening for sure," I said. "We'd better get back to the dressing rooms and make sure the girls are all right."

"I'll go," Frank replied. "You stay here—if they

bust into the theater, drop down and keep them occupied till I get back."

"How will you know I need you?"

"Bang three times on the shaft—the sound will travel."

"Good plan," I said. "And you do the same if anything's shaking on the other end."

"Will do." He took off, shimmying away into the darkness.

I got back to monitoring the main theater. Shakira was down there, covered with diamond jewelry from the tiara on her head to the ankle bracelets on her legs. In between were several bracelets, a pendant necklace, a brooch on each lapel, a pair of incredible earrings—plus a navel ring, a nose ring, and rings on most of her fingers. The diamonds alone must have weighed ten pounds!

Meanwhile, Carrera was lovingly describing each item while Shakira moved up and down the runway, showing the items off to all potential bidders and to the many people who'd come just to gawk.

Soon the bidding began. One by one, each item was bid on, bought, and cataloged by assistants.

It took a mere thirty minutes before every diamond on Shakira was claimed. With a big smile and a wave, she blew kisses to the crowd, then walked back down the runway and exited stage left.

"Don't worry, folks, she'll be back soon, covered in another set of even more fabulous gems!" Carrera said, smiling broadly. "In the meantime, here's the world's most beautiful woman—with the possible exception of Shakira, that is—Ms. Naomi Dowd!"

The crowd erupted, hooting and hollering and standing up to stare, while the spotlights searched the stage right entrance.

But nobody appeared.

"Ms. Naomi Dowd!" Carrera repeated, to more applause and shouts of approval.

Still nothing. The spotlights circled in vain. Naomi Dowd was nowhere in sight.

A uniformed security woman trotted onto the stage from the opposite side and went up to Carrera, whispering something in his ear.

His smile vanished. "What do you mean?" he asked her, forgetting that his microphone was still live. "Well, where is she? She can't have disappeared into thin air!"

I hadn't heard Frank banging three times—but I started in his direction immediately.

I didn't need three knocks to know that there was trouble ahead.

9.
The Heist

It felt like forever till I got to the spot over the dressing room. I was sure I'd arrive to find Naomi lying dead on the ground. Luckily, as I got closer, I heard her voice.

She was okay—but that didn't mean she was out of danger.

She was talking to someone. I stopped crawling long enough to identify the other voice: Bobo's. Good—she had some protection, at least. I decided to take a quick peek, then find the nearest exit from the air shaft and get down to her as soon as possible.

"How do I look?" she was asking.

"I dunno," Bobo said. "It's kinda blinding, if you ask me."

"Oh, Bobo," she said, "come on—I need an

honest opinion. Should I wear the brooch like this? Or should I pin it lower, like . . . this?"

"Babe, you know better than I do. I'm just a thug, y'know? Doin' my job. Which doesn't include beauty advice."

I was staring down at them by this time. Naomi was totally covered in jewels.I thought of knocking on the grate and telling Bobo to unscrew it so I could drop down, but something held me back. Lucky thing, too—if I'd done that, I'd never have seen what I saw, and we'd never have cracked the case.

Just as I was about to knock on the grate, I remembered the signal Joe and I had arranged. I didn't want Joe to think I was knocking for him, so I hesitated.

As I considered my options, there was a knock on the dressing-room door.

"Who is it?" Naomi called.

"You're wanted onstage, Ms. Dowd." A man's deep voice . . . with some kind of accent . . .

Filipino!

"Coming," she said. "Bobo, open the door for me, will you?"

As he reached for the knob, the door burst open, and four people—men, I guessed—wearing gas masks and dressed in black, came through the

89

doorway. Three of them had guns, but it was the fourth, the one with the sprayer, who stopped Bobo dead in his tracks before he could put his fighting skills to work.

Whatever they were spraying, it worked fast. Naomi drooped into two of the men's arms and they sat her down in a chair. I probably would have been knocked out too, except that the gas seemed to be hugging the ground, not rising my way.

Two of the intruders tied Bobo's hands and feet with duct tape, while the other two removed all of Naomi's jewelry.

"Okay!" the one who'd gassed Bobo and Naomi said in his accented voice. "I'll wait for Shakira— you go get the rest of the diamonds and I'll meet you back in the hall."

"No," said another of the gang, stepping forward and pulling out a gun. "Leave Shakira to me."

The first guy put an arm out and grabbed the second's gun hand.

"Don't worry," said the second guy. "I'm not gonna hurt her."

The guy's gun hand didn't look too steady—it was shaking a lot, in fact—so maybe he was nervous.

I fidgeted quietly, hoping Joe was on his way. I hoped he'd figured out by now that knocking three times was a pretty stupid plan. If I'd knocked—if

I'd made any sound at all—these guys would have shot the air duct, and me, full of holes.

The four thieves split up out in the hallway. I had to choose which way to go. Number two had said he wouldn't hurt Shakira, but I couldn't trust that. Joe might not be in time to save her himself. Besides, I had a better chance of overpowering one crook than three of them armed with knockout gas.

But Plan A didn't work out after all. By the time I got myself turned in the right direction, crook number two was out of sight. Which way had he gone? Where would he wait for Shakira in ambush?

I knew I'd never find them in time, so I knocked three times (finally!), turned back around, and headed for a location where I knew there'd be action: the exhibit hall.

I wondered how the thieves had gotten through the security cordon, with its camera systems and its motion detectors wired to alarms. Then I remembered the trucks, from three different companies— these guys had been fooling with those systems all day long!

I reached the grating overlooking the exhibit hall. There was a layer of gas floating along the floor here, too—anything less than seven feet tall was inside the cloud. As it began to clear, I saw the bodies of seven security personnel sprawled out cold on the floor.

The thieves didn't seem concerned about tripping the motion alarms, and it was easy to see why—there were no laser beams anywhere. All those red points of light I'd seen that morning were nowhere in sight.

Still, there were those special glass cases. Because of their extra-tough plastic backing, it would take these guys half an hour, at least, to hammer through them—time enough for security to foil the robbery.

Right?

Number two returned.

"Did you find Shakira?" asked the guy I had pegged as Sanguillen.

Number two stuck his shaking hand in his jacket pocket and pulled out a fistful of diamonds. "Found her," he said.

What had they done to her?

"We don't have much time," said Sanguillen, or whoever he was. "Any minute the cops will realize what's up. Then they'll all be down here like monkeys on a banana, and there won't be enough gas for all of them. Get to work!"

One of the others fished a sledgehammer out of his backpack.

Good luck, I thought, picturing him hacking away in frustration until the police arrived.

But then, another one of the gang took something else out of his backpack—a nail gun. He aimed it at one of the cases and shot a nail straight into the glass.

"This is the beauty part, Mr. S.," he said to the guy with the accent. "The heat of the nail gun melts the plastic backing, so you can hammer right through the glass. That's how Shakey pulled off the job at the Getty Museum last year."

I'd heard about the Getty heist, but didn't know Shakey Twist was involved. Nothing was ever brought to court—as usual.

This looked every bit like a collaboration between the Twist mob and the warlord Carlos Sanguillen. Between them, they'd thought of everything— except me and Joe.

Unfortunately, there was nothing I could do at the moment. True, there was an exit ladder straight ahead of me. But if I went down there now, I'd only be able to fight as long as I could hold my breath.

I had no choice but to act as a silent witness. The thieves smashed every case in the hall in the space of three minutes. Just as they finished, with the gas dissipating, footsteps sounded in the distance, along with a lot of shouting and coughing.

The gas wasn't powerful enough any longer to

knock the police and security guys out, but it was still good enough to slow them down—just long enough for the thieves to make their getaway.

I lowered myself down the ladder in time to see the last of them running down the dark hallway and out an emergency exit. No alarm sounded—naturally.

Never mind, I told myself as the convention center's protectors arrived on the scene. We'd have the tapes in the control room and me as a witness to back them up.

All of us were coughing, even though the gas had pretty much disappeared. My eyes burned, and the lights were suddenly way too bright.

Chief Collig burst into the hall. "What the—?" In one sweeping glance, he took in all the shattered and empty display cases.

Hal Harris and Vincent Carrera were right behind him. "The diamonds!" Carrera was shouting hysterically, over and over again. "The diamonds!"

Harris put a hand on Carrera's shoulder. "Take it easy—the police will get your diamonds back for you."

Carrera glared back at him. "That's very comforting," he said sarcastically, "coming from a man like you, who was just telling me this morning how impregnable your convention center was."

That remark caught Harris right in the gut. "We're dealing with some pretty savvy crooks here," Chief Collig put in.

"You mean Carlos Sanguillen?" I asked.

The chief looked at me, startled. "Frank Hardy. I thought you and Joe were providing extra security. Where were you when the diamonds were stolen?"

"We were . . . we were tracking the robbers' movements," I said.

"And?"

"We, um . . . we were stuck in the air ducts," I had to admit.

"I see. Nice job."

Ouch.

"Now, what makes you say Sanguillen's involved?"

"Well, he was here tonight, wasn't he?"

The chief could not have looked more surprised. "Not to my knowledge," he said. "Are you saying you actually saw him here?"

"He was right in the back of the theater during the first part of the show," I said.

"Impossible!" Chief Collig snorted. Then he seemed to reconsider. "My men weren't inside the theater, of course; we wanted to leave that to center security—" He looked over at Harris and frowned. "But obviously, we were right outside the building, keeping a tight perimeter. Sanguillen must have been heavily disguised when he got through."

"Not if he came in through the air ducts," I pointed out. "I just crawled through some of them myself to get here."

"Huh?"

"Sanguillen, and whoever else was with him, could have gotten in the building and then hidden in the ducts until it was time to strike."

"No way," Harris said. "Our cameras would have spotted them."

"Well," said the chief, "we'll have to go up to the control room and check the tapes."

At that moment there was a thumping sound over our heads, and then Joe came down the ladder from the air duct. "The diamonds?" he asked.

"Gone," I said. "I got here too late."

"Naomi?"

"She's out cold, along with Bobo and every security guard in the area."

"Dang!" I could tell Joe was was angry—but the guys he wanted to bust were already long gone.

10.
The Aftermath

"Where's Shakira?" I asked. My job was to protect her, and I'd failed miserably.

"I'm here."

I wheeled around, and there she was, still in the shimmering gown she'd worn onstage. However, she was missing every single diamond she'd had on.

"He had a gun," she explained. "I had no choice but to give him everything."

"Just one guy?" Chief Collig asked her.

"Yes."

Shakira seemed really calm, considering what had just happened to her. Most girls would have been totally shaken up, but not her. Either she was really cool under pressure, or she knew something she wasn't telling. I hoped it was the first—I kind of liked her, and I would have hated to think anything bad about her. But her reaction *did* seem strange.

I wondered if Chief Collig had noticed. If he had, he wasn't letting on. He just kept taking notes, nodding his head as she told everyone how she'd been ambushed on her way back to her dressing room.

"He had a gun," she repeated. "I don't know what kind. I just let him take the diamonds."

"And you never saw his face?" Chief Collig asked.

"No, he had a gas mask on," Shakira said.

"But you didn't smell any gas."

"No."

"And he didn't spray gas at you."

"No."

Chief Collig looked at Hal Harris and raised an eyebrow. "That's interesting," he said, "because they knocked everyone else out with gas."

If Shakira was rattled, she didn't show it. She just shrugged and said, "I already told you, it was a gun. You know, the kind that shoots bullets."

Officer Con Reilly walked over to Chief Collig. "Chief," he said, "the control boxes for the alarms and motion detectors have all been tampered with."

"Mmm," said the chief. "Definitely a well-planned,

professional job. Just like we were afraid of." He shook his head in frustration. "I wish the feds had gotten involved when I asked them to."

"You called the FBI?" Harris asked, surprised.

"I did," the chief said, "but they said they had bigger fish to fry."

I could tell he was upset. A major robbery had succeeded right under his nose, blackening the reputation of the Bayport Police Department.

Of course, without more sophisticated help, the chief really couldn't be blamed for not stopping the robbery. If the mob had joined with Carlos Sanguillen to pull it off, they would have had much better technology than the local police and security combined. And Frank and I hadn't been able to prevent the crime either. We'd all failed—but I wasn't ready to admit defeat. Not yet, anyway.

"Well, let's see what the videotapes tell us," Chief Collig said. "Mr. Harris, if you'd be so kind as to lead us to the control room? In the meantime, Officer Reilly, please make sure everyone present stays put. Nobody's to leave the building until I say so."

"Er, Chief . . . ?" Reilly began.

"Yes?" the chief barked. He was definitely *not* in a good mood.

"What about food and drink? I mean, it's gonna be awhile till we take statements from everyone, right?"

"All night, probably," the chief agreed. "Call the diner and have them bring over some dinner. They're open all night, anyway." Then he turned to Shakira. "I'd like you to stay too, please."

"I already told you all I know!" she complained. "And where am I supposed to wait? Out there in the theater with that crowd of people?"

The chief sighed. "Okay, you can stay in your dressing room. But don't go anywhere until we're done with you."

"When will that be?" she asked.

"Whenever we say," he shot back. "Mr. Harris? Lead on."

Harris gave me a wary look. "Are you sure it's okay, Chief? I mean, to leave these folks here unsupervised?" I knew he meant me and Frank, but I couldn't blame him for doubting us after what had just happened.

"They're all right," Chief Collig assured him. "We go back a long way—believe me, they're the least of our worries."

As soon as they were out of sight, Shakira reached for my arm. "Joe?"

"It's okay," I assured her. "It's all over now. You're safe."

She looked down, and I saw her shudder slightly. "I . . . I could have . . . he could have . . ."

"I know. It's okay now. You're going to be fine."

"What happened to you, Joe? Where did you go?"

"I'm . . . I'm sorry, Shakira. I should have been there with you when—"

"I could've been killed."

"I know . . . I'm sorry. Look, I've really got to go investigate. But I'll be right back, okay?"

"That's what you said the last time." She went off to her dressing room, leaning against the wall as she went. She seemed bummed—but probably not more bummed than I was. My chances of going out with her were shrinking by the second.

I turned and saw Frank standing there. Great. He'd seen the whole thing go down with Shakira. That made me feel even worse.

"Man, she's tough," he said.

"Tell me about it."

Frank and I exchanged glances. We were both dying to see what was on those tapes. On the other hand, who was going to track the thieves' escape route? And what about Naomi and Bobo?

"So, what do we do first?" I asked.

"The girls," he answered. "They're our assignment. Let's keep it simple."

"Huh?"

"Chief Collig will tell us what's on the tapes. If the mob, or Sanguillen, was behind this—and it sure looks that way—the police are better equipped to round them up than we are."

That was true.

"Then what use are we?" I asked.

"Joe, my instincts tell me those thieves succeeded way too easily."

"Meaning?"

"Meaning they had to have someone on the inside, helping them."

"Someone on the inside? Like who?"

"That's what we're here to find out. But right now, let's make sure the girls are all right."

I walked with him to Naomi's dressing room. She was sitting slumped over in her makeup chair, massaging her temples. She looked like she was going to heave any second.

Bobo was in even worse shape, curled up on the floor, groaning like he'd been punched hard in the gut.

Whatever gas the thieves had used, it had faded away quickly—and it must have been heavier than air, or it would have gone up into the air ducts and knocked me and Frank out too.

"I saw the criminals burst in here, Joe," Frank said as he mopped Naomi's brow with a cold washcloth. He proceeded to tell me everything he'd seen, from the gas masks to the nail gun.

"Man, those guys came prepared," I said. Still, considering that the police and security knew something was coming, Frank was right—it had been way too easy.

I knelt down next to Bobo. "You okay?"

"I'm great," he said, opening one bloodshot eye. "Fantastic. Never been better."

"Sorry. Anything I can do to help?"

"Water . . ."

I got him some, and he sat up . . . sort of. "Ugghh. I think I'm gonna blow chunks."

"Please don't," Naomi begged him, covering her own mouth. "Don't even talk about it."

Frank was still patting her down with that cold washcloth. His other hand was massaging the back of her neck.

"So tell me, Bobo," I said, switching topics, "I hear you did time in Sing Sing."

That woke him up. He opened his other eye and shot me a killer glance. "Are you saying I was part of this?" he said, grabbing my shirt.

I didn't back down. "I'm not saying anything. Why don't you let go of me?"

He pushed me off, but he did let go. "I'm strictly legal now, man," he said. "I turned a corner. I'm never gonna see the inside of that place again."

"Bobo's telling the truth," Naomi said. "I knew

all about his past when I hired him, because he told me before I even asked. He's totally loyal to me, I promise you."

"All right," Frank said. "Tell me something, Bobo. You've been in prison. You've spent years with the kind of people who pulled off this heist. Could you know some of them?"

"I might," he said. "But that doesn't mean I was working with 'em."

"Of course not," Frank said. "Still, it's possible the police might get curious about it—if they felt you weren't being helpful."

Bobo grunted. "Like I said, I might know one of 'em."

"One with a foreign accent?" Frank asked.

Bobo looked confused. "Foreign accent? You mean, like, Spanish?"

"No. More like Filipino."

"I wouldn't know that accent even if I heard it," Bobo said. "All the guys in Sing Sing were Americans. English speakers, some Spanish, that was it. But I did recognize one of the others."

Frank and I came to instant attention.

"Are you sure?" Frank said. "They knocked you unconscious pretty quickly."

"Not before I saw that hand shaking," Bobo said,

his expression darkening. "I'd know that guy any-where, mask or no mask."

He looked straight at Frank and added, "Why do you think they call him Shakey Twist?"

SUSPECT PROFILE

<u>Name:</u> Shakey Twist

<u>Hometown:</u> Atlantic City, New Jersey

<u>Physical description:</u> Age 34, 5', 11", 200 lbs. Pencil-thin mustache, horrible scar on left cheek. Snarling expression, scary dude, even though he doesn't look very physically menacing. He'd just as soon kill you as look at you.

<u>Occupation:</u> High-ranking mobster in his home town. The other dons down there regularly kiss his ring. Involved in all kinds of rackets, but diamonds aren't exactly new to him, and he's pulled off quite a few complicated heists—none of which he's ever been nailed for.

<u>Background:</u> Son of a con man, he learned well from his daddy and rose in the ranks of the A.C. mob. Unlike many of his fellows, he had the smarts to avoid serving time in prison—until he was finally caught for jaywalking and tax evasion. He was released just a year later (money buys the best lawyers) and is once again the guy New Jersey cops would most like to nail.

<u>Suspicious behavior</u>: E-mails indicate that he and his guys were plotting to steal the diamonds from the Bayport Convention Center. Was photographed meeting in Antwerp with Philippine warlord/terrorist Carlos Sanguillen.

<u>Suspected of</u>: Being the brains behind, or at least providing the personnel for, the heist. He's connected to both Shakira and Bobo Hines, so either one of them could have been in on it with him, working from the inside.

<u>Possible motive</u>: You can never be too rich—or too evil.

There was nothing more either of them could tell us right now, and anyway, the identity of the thieves was becoming pretty clear. So Frank and I excused ourselves, explaining that we wanted to check around for clues.

Frank went to examine the thieves' escape route while I went back to see Shakira. Now that Bobo had identified Shakey Twist as one of the robbers, I was going to have to ask her some hard questions. After all, she was the only person who had an encounter with one of the robbers and stayed awake to tell about it. It looked very much like Shakira was in this thing up to her pretty little neck.

I found her in her dressing room, and right away,

I knew something was different. She'd changed from her show gown back into street clothes—stylish jeans and a tank top with sandals—but it wasn't just her outfit that I noticed right off the bat.

Her whole attitude was different. Before, she'd been tough but flirty—definitely in a good mood. Now she was more like a cat who'd been scared within an inch of its life.

"About time you showed up," she commented as I entered the dressing room. "You're some lame bodyguard, let me tell you."

"Sorry," I said. "I got chloroformed."

"Oh, really? Well, that takes skill."

Man, she was really being harsh!

"Hey, I didn't do it on purpose," I said.

"Well, forget it," she said. "It doesn't matter now. It's all over now, isn't it? The crooks pulled it off and made you guys look silly. Not much more to say, is there?"

"I guess. But maybe my brother and I can nail these guys yet—with your help."

"*My* help?" She laughed, but I could tell she didn't really think it was funny. "What am I supposed to do, wrestle down a bunch of guys with guns?"

"You might start by telling me everything that happened, from the time you left the stage till the time the police showed up."

"Haven't I already done that once? I'm sick of reminding myself."

"You never know," I said. "Sometimes you leave out something the first time—some small detail that winds up being really important."

Shakira sighed. "Oh, all right, but I'm telling you, you're wasting your time. I was walking back to my dressing room—you know, to take off the jewelry, get changed into my next gown, and put on the next bunch of items to sell—when this guy steps in front of me, points a gun in my face, and says, 'Okay, babe, off with the jewels.' "

"He called you 'babe'?"

"Yeah."

"And was his voice at all familiar?"

If I thought she was scared and angry before, she suddenly amped it up into hyperdrive.

"You're trying to tie me up with this, aren't you?" she said, looking at me as if she'd never seen me before.

"Not me, certainly," I said. "But the police might start leaning that way. Especially since we now have a pretty good idea of who it was." I was using one of the oldest tactics in the book to get a criminal to speak: pretending I knew exactly who organized the crime, even though my evidence was a bit . . . shaky.

"Well, if that's true, why don't the police just arrest him?"

"I'm sure they would, if they could find him. But something tells me he won't be staying in this country for very long. Maybe you have some idea where he might go."

She picked up a hand mirror and threw it against the wall, shattering it. "I could have been killed, do you realize that? No thanks to the police *or* you!"

"Did he actually threaten you?"

"You think he wouldn't have killed me if I hadn't handed the diamonds over? He was in a *major* hurry."

"I'm sure he was." And, in fact, I had to wonder why he hadn't just sprayed Shakira with whatever gas he'd used on everyone else. I wanted to ask her, but she was already mad enough.

Maybe, just maybe, her ex-boyfriend Shakey had wanted to talk to her one more time before he disappeared for a while.

Or maybe Shakira had never really broken up with him. Maybe she was his little secret for the past three months—the ace up his sleeve.

Well, she sure wasn't going to admit to that. Not yet, anyway.

I excused myself and found Frank. "Find anything?" I asked.

"No, but I didn't go outside."

"Why not?"

"It's crawling with police out there," he said.

"Where were they when the thieves were pulling off the robbery?" I wondered.

"Probably watching the show on all those big screens in the hallways. Checking out Shakira in all those diamonds, just like everyone else."

"The perfect distraction," I agreed. "That's how Sanguillen could come and go without being noticed."

"Human nature, I guess," Frank said. "Who could ignore Shakira? Certainly not you, Joe."

"Shut up, you dog," I retorted. "Like you're not being a total fool about Naomi Dowd."

When we entered the control room, everyone was looking as down as could be. On the monitor, there was an old-time cartoon playing—one where clever cat thieves were being pursued by dumb dog police.

"What was on the security tapes?" I asked, confused.

"You're lookin' at it," Harris said. "Seven cameras out back, covering a whole sector of the convention center, had their tapes switched sometime late this afternoon."

"I'm not surprised," I said. "I got chloroformed trying to check that out."

"There were trucks around from a New York

City–based company," Frank added. "I saw them before I . . . before I got jumped from behind and sent to la-la land."

"This is an absolute disaster!" Carrera said. "Why didn't I insist on a Manhattan theater? The NYPD would never have let themselves be made fools of like this." He was near tears over the loss of his precious diamonds and the wreck of his big show.

"Gas was the Twist mob's weapon of choice last year when they robbed the Getty Museum," Chief Collig said.

I saw Frank take a seat in front of a computer and key in some commands. "What are you doing?" I asked.

"Searching Shakey Twist," he said. "Check this out—three Interpol sightings just this past week. Manila, Antwerp, then Atlantic City."

"Sounds like he and Sanguillen have been keeping company lately," I said.

"It's an open-and-shut case," Chief Collig said. "Trouble is, these guys are geniuses at getting away with it. Sanguillen has escaped from prison as many times as Shakey Twist has been found not guilty."

11.
Dead Men Tell No Tales

The police were just finishing up outside and heading back in to interview the many witnesses.

"They've been all over it by now," I said to Joe, not too hopeful of finding anything.

"Sure they have. And now it's our turn."

Bright floodlights were focused on the emergency exit, and on the path leading from it to the road and the bay. Yellow crime-scene tape was strung between trees and light poles, fencing off an area that was being still being combed by dozens of police. Convention center security stood by, watching and keeping away curious passersby.

I looked across the road to the convention center

marina. Dozens of boats were bobbing in the water. Speedboats and yachts, and sailboats with their sails wound tightly around their masts.

"They must have gotten away by boat," I said. "There's no way they could have driven out of here without going through the center's guarded gates."

Joe and I walked down the path, past Chief Collig. "Find anything, Chief?" I asked.

"Shoe prints—seven sets. They must have had three men covering the exit from outside."

"Nothing else?"

"Not yet," he said through gritted teeth. "I think we're going to do the interviews and pack it in for the night. I'll leave a few men on watch detail, and we'll come back in the morning. The floodlights are good, but it's not the same as daylight."

Joe and I kept walking, crossing the road and moving onto the docks of the marina. Two police officers passed us going the other way, their walkie-talkies pressed to their ears. I recognized one of them as Officer Bart Edwards. "Right, Chief," he was saying. "We'll be right there."

"Excuse me, Bart," I said. "Did anyone search these boats?"

"Every one of them," he answered. "They're all clean and clear."

"Hmm. Thanks. Mind if we have a look around anyway?"

"Fine by me—just don't touch anything that looks like evidence."

After he'd gone, Joe and I walked each of the docks. Obviously, the police had decided there wasn't anything here left to find. Maybe they were right—there certainly was nothing obvious.

Frank and I weren't even sure what we were looking for, but we both felt that the crooks had to have come and gone this way. And when people come and go—even experienced professionals—they sometimes leave clues behind.

"But surely the police would have found it, whatever it was," you might say.

Ah, but you know how people are. They only find what they're *looking* for. Joe and I weren't looking for any particular thing. Trust me, it's the best way to find something important.

A coast guard boat sped by, its floodlights scanning the bay for any signs of the thieves. It turned sharply to avoid hitting the marina, and sent up a big wake that soon had us grabbing onto the pilings to avoid getting thrown into the water.

"Hey!" I said, getting to my feet again and seeing if I was wet anywhere.

"They really should learn to—hey, Frank, what's that?"

Joe was pointing to the water, where something was protruding from under the dock.

I squinted my eyes, trying to see the object—and I quickly realized what it was. "Joe," I said, "it's a mask. A gas mask—with a body attached."

12.

The Worm Turns

We decided to do a little investigating on our own before involving any authorities.

We fished him out of the water and hauled him onto the dock, grunting every inch of the way. Water gushed out of his mouth, nose, and ears. It poured from the pockets of his jacket—along with a shiny object. I picked it up with two fingers and held it up to the light.

It was a diamond ring—one any woman would want for her engagement—in a fancy carved gold setting with a gold band. I pocketed this piece of evidence, then pulled the guy's gas mask off while Frank checked his pulse.

"Long gone," he said.

"Maybe this is why," I said, pointing to a neat round hole in the flak jacket, just over the chest area. "I'd say it was a .38 caliber. One clean shot, from the front." I paused. "Why do you think he was killed?"

"I don't know. Maybe they—the leaders of this robbery—caught him stashing away some of the loot for himself. Maybe he was a hired gun," Frank guessed.

I shook my head. "Then what's this ring doing in his pocket? Wouldn't they have taken it back?"

"They probably shot him when they found the first thing he'd taken. My guess is he hit the water before they had a chance to really pat him down."

"And killing him had the added benefit of one less person to share the loot with," I pointed out.

"True." Frank had his hand deep inside the dead guy's pants pocket. "Something else in here," he said, just before fishing out a soaking-wet business card. "Aha!"

"Can you read it?" I asked.

He squinted, holding it up to the floodlight that illuminated this part of the dock. "It's a diamond firm in New York City . . . something with a G . . ."

"Let me see that," I said, trying to grab it from him.

"Eh, eh, eh!" he said, yanking it away just in time. "Don't finger the merchandise."

"You know I've got better eyes than you do."

"Says who?"

I grabbed it from him and read it out loud. "'Glickstein Jewelers, Nathan Glickstein, President. One-fifty-five West Forty-seventh Street, seventh floor.'"

"It might be nothing," Frank said.

"I'll bet you everything I own it isn't," I responded.

"Maybe you're right," he said. "It's a good bet those thieves will go there to try and fence their big haul."

"When?"

"As soon as possible," he said.

"That would be tomorrow morning."

"Sunday?"

"They're open on Sunday, closed on Saturday," I told him.

"How do you know that?"

"It says so on the card, bro," I said with a smile, handing it back to him. "Maybe you should get your eyes checked. Turns out they're not so great after all."

Frank frowned, but he had no comeback. He got right back down to business, checking to see if the guy had any ID on him. There was none—no surprise. Why would somebody who was going to rob a place carry ID, and do the cops a favor?

We called the police over, showed them the body, then went back inside the center. "I want to search Glickstein on the Internet," Frank said.

That was cool by me. I was as curious as he was.

The police had been busy while we were gone. We arrived at the hall where the witness interviews were being conducted, to find that almost all the security personnel who'd been gassed were already gone. Chief Collig was just leaving, on his way out to examine the body.

"Anything I should know before I go out there and check out the stiff?" he asked us.

Frank and I exchanged a quick glance. Neither of us was sure whether to mention the ring or the business card we'd found on the corpse. Our intuition told both of us that they held the key to something important, but I don't think either of us was ready to give up our own investigation.

"Not really," Frank said. "Where are Naomi and Shakira?"

"We're done with them," the chief said. "They're being put up at the Bay View Hotel for the night, with a guard posted at each of their doors for protection."

"Great," Frank said. "Thanks, Chief. Good job."

There he went, buttering up Chief Collig. Frank and I both knew he'd be incredibly mad if he knew we were concealing the ring and the business card we'd found. We'd be sure to turn them over to the police as soon as we were done with them, though. And the chief might be a little less furious because Frank had buttered him up beforehand.

Don't get me wrong—the chief's a great guy, and a very good police officer. He's just a lousy detective. He can follow up a clue just fine, but the intuition you need to be an investigator has never been his strong point.

Right now, the Bayport police would be totally focused on rounding up Carlos Sanguillen and Shakey Twist. That, and identifying the corpse, would keep them busy for a while. Too busy to check out Glickstein Jewelers, which could be a false lead, amounting to nothing—and which Frank and I could easily handle for them.

We found Hal Harris in the control room and asked to borrow one of his computers. He led us to a side cubicle, keyed in a password, and presto—we were online. Frank searched "Nathan Glickstein" and "Jewelers," and up came the correct address in New York City. We linked to the firm's website, but it was just ordinary stuff.

Then we went down the search results a little deeper, and found a newspaper article from the *New York Times* dated 1998—when a man named Nathan Glickstein was found innocent of fencing diamonds. Bingo!

Farther down in the article, it mentioned whose diamonds he'd been accused of fencing: *Carlos Sanguillen's*. Apparently he'd been charged with etching ID numbers on illegally mined diamonds, then selling them as legit ones. The indictment also accused him of associating with mobsters in Atlantic City, although it didn't name any names.

"That's it!" Frank gasped. "They're going to dump the stolen goods with Glickstein! Joe, we've got to get down there right away."

It all seemed to add up—Sanguillen, Twist, Glickstein.

Except for one thing: a dead man floating in the water with a diamond ring in his pocket.

We walked back to Frank's bike and rode home. It was three a.m. when we got to bed. Frank set his alarm for six in the morning. "Three hours' sleep?" I moaned.

"You know we've got to get to Glickstein early, the theives have a head start on us as it is," he said. "Once they get him the diamonds, it's all over. Nothing will ever be proven, and they'll get off scot-free again, just like they've done every time so far."

"Yeah," Frank said, "but don't you think one of us should stay behind and keep an eye on the girls?"

"Hmmm. Do you think that's really necessary, Frank? I mean, they're under police guard. They're not going anywhere. And with the diamonds already stolen, what's the risk to them?"

"Well, for one thing, Shakira's the only witness who got a look at her attacker."

Whoa, major role reversal. Was Frank confusing the evidence because of a girl? "No, she wasn't," I said. "Remember Bobo recognizing Shakey? Besides, the guy Shakira recognized was wearing a gas mask, dude. Think she could ever pick him out of a lineup? I doubt it."

"Still. Our mission from ATAC says—"

"Oh, can it, bro. I see right through you. Why don't you stay here and hang out with Naomi, and I'll go to New York. Just do me one favor, okay? Peek in on Shakira every once in awhile."

"It's not like that, Joe," he started.

"Right. Sure it isn't. Go to sleep, okay? Looking out for Naomi Dowd is tough work."

I kind of wished it was *me* staying behind with the girls. Before Shakira ran into the middle of a diamond heist, I was pretty sure she'd been at least a little interested in me. But I'd left her alone to defend herself during the robbery, and she hadn't forgiven me for that. I could totally understand where she was coming from. Still, tomorrow would have been a good day to try and make it up to her.

That may have been what Frank had in mind with Naomi—only he'd have to get around Bobo first. I don't know why I took pity on Frank and offered to go to New York by myself, but I did.

I just hoped I didn't regret it later.

SUSPECT PROFILE

Name: Nathan Glickstein

Hometown: New York, NY

Physical description: Age 70, 5', 5", wild gray hair, bad posture.

Occupation: Diamond buyer/seller/appraiser (and fencer). He's got two sets of books—one for his legitimate business, and one for . . . well, you know.

Background: Son of a peddler, he started out gypping customers at an early age. From the time he entered the diamond business, he began figuring out ways to up his profits by being smarter than everybody else. Unfortunately, some

of his smart friends turned out to be wiseguys—
including Shakey Twist, among others. It was on
a business trip to the Philippines that he was
approached by Carlos Sanguillen, who convinced
Glickstein to fence his illegal diamonds. This
secret arrangement worked well until Sanguillen
became one of the world's most wanted terror-
ists. His high jinks nearly landed Glickstein in
jail. Lucky thing his friend Shakey knew some
good lawyers!

Suspicious behavior: His card in the pocket of
the dead body's jacket.

Suspected of: Being the fence for the diamonds
Shakey and Sanguillen stole.

Possible motive: Beyond getting even richer? The
pleasure of outsmarting everybody. And that
means EVERYBODY.

The door was locked, but there was a button to
push. I pushed it, and a buzzer sounded, freeing the
lock and allowing me inside the office of Nathan
Glickstein Jewelers.

"Can I help you?"

An old man looked up at me from his chair. He'd
been bent over a microscope, or something very

much like one. Now he looked up at me, with a pair of Coke-bottle-thick glasses perched on his nose and a wild gray head of hair erupting in every direction out of his head.

His "office" was not really much of an office at all. It was a tiny room behind a frosted glass door on the seventh floor of an enormous building, full of dozens of offices just like it, all buying and selling diamonds.

Glickstein Jewelers was divided in half by a counter, behind which sat Mr. Glickstein himself. The back half of the office was crammed with shelves, all stacked with boxes, files, loose papers, and dust.

On my side of the partition was a bare floor, with two chairs for anyone waiting his turn. Both chairs were empty. It was ten in the morning, but I had the feeling they were empty just about all the time. Whatever business got done here, not much of it was person-to-person, or retail—and probably not legal, either.

"Nathan Glickstein?"

"That's me. And you are?"

"Joe. Joe Hardy, sir."

"What do you want, Joe Hardy? You want to sell me something? Because you don't look like the type who buys."

"I'm not selling anything. I'm just—sir, could I ask you something?"

"Why not?" He was curious now, tilting his head down so he could see me through the top half of his bifocals.

"Has Carlos Sanguillen shown up here today?"

That got him. I saw him flinch noticeably. He pushed his glasses farther up his nose and stood up. "I don't know anyone by that name."

"Shakey Twist? Do you know him?"

"No, I don't. And where did you say you were from?"

I saw him reach for something under the counter. "Sir, I wouldn't do that if I were you. I'm not a police officer, and I'm not here to arrest you or anything."

"Arrest me? Arrest me for what?" He didn't move back from whatever he'd been about to reach for—but he didn't move any closer, either.

"You know about the diamond theft in Bayport last night?"

"I read it in the paper this morning. So?"

"Both men who've been named as suspects have ties to you."

"Baloney. That's pure baloney! Who sent you, huh?"

Baloney? What century was this guy from? "I sent

myself, sir. You wouldn't be about to fence those stolen diamonds, would you?"

"I have no idea what you're talking about, young fella. And you'd better get out of here now, before I call for security."

"Just one more question. Did you know they've already killed one of their buddies who helped out on the heist?"

That made him go white. "I guess that didn't make it in time for the morning papers, huh?" I continued.

He looked at me like I'd just arrived from Mars.

"I'd be careful if I were you, sir," I said as I backed slowly toward the door. "These are dangerous guys you're dealing with. If they killed one of their friends, they could easily kill another. You might want to come clean before it's too late."

His mouth opened, but he didn't say anything. He just stood there, frozen in place, staring at me.

"Okay, I can understand if you don't want to tell me. I mean, who am I, right? Tell you what—why don't you just call the NYPD? They'll protect you, sir. And if you help them nail Shakey Twist and Carlos Sanguillen, I'll bet there'd even be a reward in it for you."

I hit the elevator button and waited. And waited. When it finally came, the door opened to reveal two men. They were standing side by side, their hands together in front of their stomachs. They were Asian—in fact, they could easily have been Filipino—and they looked dangerous. They stared at me with raised eyebrows.

Man, I thought. *Mr. Glickstein must have pushed that panic button the moment I'd left his office, because they sure had gotten here quick.*

"I . . . think I'll take the stairs," I said, backing away slowly.

The elevator door started to close. Then a hand reached out and blocked it. The doors reopened, and out stepped the pair of thugs. They came right for me, reaching inside their jackets for the guns that were no doubt hidden there.

I turned and ran for my life. Reaching the stairway just in time, I raced down the steps, jumping them in bunches like a track star in hurdles. But I could still hear the thunk-thunk of heavy-booted feet behind me.

Somewhere around the third floor I stopped hearing them, but I kept on going as fast as I could. I reached the bottom stairwell and pushed on the exit door—and that's when the hand grabbed me by the shoulder.

It yanked me back around. I ducked instinctively, the result of years of martial arts training. As the iron fist went flying, I head-butted the thug right in the abdomen. He buckled over, and I raised my head quickly, hitting him in the nose with the back of my skull.

He staggered back into the wall and slumped to the floor, dazed and bleeding. I looked around for his buddy—you know, the one who'd been following me down the stairs—but he was nowhere in sight.

Hmmm . . . maybe he'd taken the elevator down instead and was waiting for me out there in the lobby, with a gun in his hand. . . .

Meanwhile, thug number one was on the rise again. I took him out with a swift karate kick to the jaw. Then I searched his pockets, finding nothing but a big black Beretta pistol. I took it, flung open the door to the lobby, and ducked to avoid the bullets I expected to come.

To my surprise, the lobby was empty. The footsteps chasing me had stopped about halfway down to the ground floor. The elevator door was open. Hmmm. That was weird.

I tried to piece things together. I'd been chased down from the seventh floor, but the footsteps chasing me died after three or four flights of stairs. If one thug had taken the elevator down to ambush me in the stairwell, where had the other one gone? Had he just left the building?

As if in answer to my question, at that very moment the door from the stairs burst open. Thug number two ran right past, without even seeing me.

"Freeze!" I yelled, leveling the pistol at him.

He froze.

"Drop the gun and turn around—slowly."

He turned around slowly, all right, but he still held the gun over his head.

"I said drop it!"

He lowered the arm with the gun, but he was still hanging onto it. *Too long*, I thought. He was going to pull a fast one any second, for sure.

I dodged to the right, just in time, rolling over once until I was safely behind a pillar.

By the time I did that, he'd fired three times in a row. I heard a groan from the stairwell, and I knew what had happened—I'd been standing right between the two thugs. Number two had just shot his buddy!

He turned to me, firing again and again. Then a click—his gun was empty. He cursed, turned, and ran for the street doors.

If I'd been a cop, I probably would have fired my weapon—at least a warning shot. But I wasn't a cop. I didn't have a license to kill. So I didn't fire.

I might have followed him to see where he led me, but I knew that would be difficult on the crowded streets of New York. Plus he might have reloaded by now, and I didn't want any innocent bystanders getting hurt.

But there was something else bothering me: If these guys had come here to kill me, then why had thug number two stopped following me down the stairs?

Only one reason—because he'd gone back *up* the stairs.

I remembered the looks on their faces when the elevator door opened and they first saw me. *Surprised.*

I got a horrible, sinking feeling that Glickstein hadn't pushed the panic button after all.

Maybe he should have.

I checked on thug number one, but it didn't take long to see that he was stone cold dead. If I hadn't ducked out of the way so fast, it would have been me.

I rode the elevator back up to the seventh floor. Glickstein's door was hanging wide open.

Not a good sign.

I went inside and peered over the counter. Nathan Glickstein was still sitting in his chair.

Only now, there was a neat round bullet hole right through the center of his forehead.

FRANK

13.
Diamonds Are Deceiving

I got to the Bay View Hotel first thing in the morning. I felt awful about letting ATAC down—and even worse about letting Naomi down. From the moment we'd first laid eyes on each other, I was sure she liked me. You know, *liked*. And you *know* I liked her.

But now I could tell things had changed. I'd deserted her while Bobo was at least on the job, even though he turned out to be worse than useless.

The reason I'd let Joe go to New York City alone? Well, I felt guilty about it, honestly. But I saw no reason why it should be a dangerous errand—unless he got to Glickstein's at the same time Twist and Sanguillen did.

What were the odds of that, anyway?

Pretty good, actually—they'd be in a hurry to unload the stolen diamonds and go into hiding until the cops got tired of looking for them. I imagined Glickstein's job was to find buyers for the stolen jewels, take his cut, and hold the rest for the criminals until it was safe for them to surface.

At least, that's what I *imagined*. So I thought it was safe to send Joe there alone and spend my day trying to keep an eye on what the Bayport police were doing, and to get back in Naomi's good book.

"Any ID on the dead guy yet?" I asked Chief Collig when I saw him in the lobby.

"Not yet," he said. "We're running prints now. I'll let you know."

"What room's Naomi in, Chief?"

"I'm not sure it's a good idea to see her right now. She's been through an ordeal—and now her bodyguard's disappeared."

"*What*? You mean Bobo—?"

"That's right. He wasn't in his room when the officers knocked with a breakfast tray for him. Then they found two other officers out cold on either end of the staircase. Bobo must have clocked them. They didn't wake up for a good half hour."

"But why would Bobo—"

"I asked myself the same thing," the chief said. "I figure he was part of the robbery. They had to have somebody on the inside, because the motion-sensor boxes were fooled with."

"But they came in from outside to do that," I told him. "They had trucks from a security company based in Atlantic City."

"A nonexistent company, probably," the chief added, scowling. "But I'm still convinced Bobo Hines was a part of it. He did time in Sing Sing with Shakey Twist, did you know that?"

I nodded. "True. But if he was in on it, then why did they knock him out with the gas?"

"Maybe he was just pretending to be knocked out, so he'd look innocent!" Chief Collig said, extremely pleased with himself.

I knew he was wrong, but I had to admit it wasn't a bad theory. "I'd still like to see Naomi, if I could," I said. "I was assigned by ATAC to protect her, after all."

He frowned, then said, "Room four-oh-five. See if you can find out anything about Bobo while you're at it."

"Sure thing, Chief. I'll do that. Oh, and what about Shakira?"

"We'll be grilling her for hours," he said. "She was Shakey Twist's girlfriend not long ago, did you know that?"

"No kidding!" I said, pretending to be surprised.

"Yes. In fact, before we learned about Bobo Hines's connection with Twist, Shakira was our main suspect as the inside man—or should I say woman. And right now, she's our only remaining link to Twist."

Naomi looked totally freaked out when she answered my knock. "Oh, it's you!" she said. "Good." She pulled me inside and shut the door behind us.

"Is it true Bobo's gone?" she asked me in a whisper.

"Yeah. They think he may have been in on the heist."

"No way was he a part of that! He and Shakey *hated* each other—they even had a fight back in Sing Sing and had to be separated."

"With this much money at stake, you'd be surprised how quickly two thieves can kiss and make up," I told her.

"Look, I know you don't like Bobo," she said. "But I'm telling you, he left because he was flipping out. He can't stand being confined—even in a hotel."

I could see how he might feel that way, but I didn't believe he'd just disappear, knowing how the police would look at it.

"Speaking of which, I need to get out of here too. I've got a show in London tomorrow night, and I want to get home first and pack some things."

"Where's home?"

"L.A."

"You want to go to L.A. just for clothes, then all the way back to London? In one day?"

"You see why I need to get out of here? Maybe you could ask Chief Whatsisname to finish questioning me. I mean, I've already told him everything I know."

"They're just waiting on some new information," I explained.

"Oh? Like what?"

"They found a dead body. One of the thieves, they think."

She didn't seem as shocked as I thought she'd be. "Oh, really? Well, that's good, isn't it? One less."

Her reaction seemed a little cold. I figured she was angry about being tied up and gassed into oblivion.

"What else have they found out?" she asked.

"Not much. The rest of the gang disappeared. The police know pretty much who they are, but it won't be easy to track them down. Some of them may already be out of the country."

"I don't think so." She was biting her lip, and her eyes were filling with tears. "Frank, there's something else," she said.

"What do you mean?" I asked, sitting next to her and taking her hand in mine.

She leaned her head in close, and her whisper got even softer, as if she thought somebody else might be close by, listening.

"They're after me, Frank."

"Huh? Who's after you?"

"Those thieves. They were after Bobo, too, but he got away before they could get him—at least, I hope he did. . . ."

"What are you talking about, Naomi? Why would the thieves be after you?"

She shrugged and sniffed back the tears. "Beats me. I guess they thought we could identify them. I don't know why they would think that—I mean, they were wearing gas masks. But I guess they aren't taking any chances."

"Where are you getting all this?" I asked. "I don't believe—"

"Oh, no? Well, check this out, then!" She whipped out her cell phone and flipped it open. Then she called up her recent text messages.

It was from "outside caller." I read it out loud. Slowly. " 'You can't escape us. Say your prayers.' "

"Who sent this?" I asked.

"The thieves, obviously. Frank, I'm terrified. If I can get out of town and disappear for a while, until they've rounded up all the thieves, then everything will be all right. Or, at least, I think it will."

"So that London show. . . ?"

"Yeah—I made it up."

"Naomi, you can trust me," I said, brushing her hair away from her face.

"Bobo's gone," she said. "Will you protect me until it's safe?"

"You know I will."

I don't know what made me say that. I guess I was just blinded by her beauty or something. I mean, I had school starting the next day! Even if I took a few days off, it wouldn't be enough. It would take the police much longer than that to roll up Shakey Twist's whole operation, never mind Sanguillen, who was probably on an airplane to some foreign land already.

"Oh, thank you, Frank—thank you! I knew I could count on you." She leaned over and kissed me on the cheek. It took my breath away. "As soon as you can get me out of here, we'll take off out of this town and get as far away as we can!"

I left her there for the moment and headed back down to the lobby. Chief Collig whistled me over. "Find out anything from her?" he asked.

"She thinks Bobo ran away because he was afraid they were going to kill him."

"That's rich," the chief said with a laugh. "Why would they do that?"

"That's what I said. Listen, Chief, she's pretty frazzled. Do you think you could release her any time soon?"

"I suppose," he said. "She's not under suspicion, after all. It's no crime to hire an ex-felon to be your bodyguard. At least, not last time I looked."

"Thanks."

"Reilly! Could you assign someone to process Ms. Dowd's release?"

"Sure, Chief," said our old friend Con Reilly, who was sitting at the hotel manager's desk, arranging reports. "I'll send someone up to let her know right away."

"Good man." Turning back to me, the chief said, "Oh, and here's something interesting for you, Frank— we got a match on the prints from the stiff."

"Oh, yeah? And?"

"It was Shakey Twist himself."

I stood there in total shock. The dead man didn't look a whole lot like the photos of Twist we'd seen. He must have had plastic surgery done on his face recently. I wondered if Shakira knew anything about that.

"I know, I can't believe it either," said the chief. "Different face, but the prints were the same. You'd think he'd have spent the extra money to do them over too."

I wandered out of the hotel and into the heat of the sunny spring day. But I was still deep in my own thoughts.

Shakey Twist had been killed by one of his own partners—right after a wildly successful robbery. I'd seen cases on TV where the boss of a mob rubs out one of his underlings, but I'd never seen it live.

The killer had to be Sanguillen, or one of his men. But why? There was no way Twist would have tried to hide a piece or two of jewelry for himself, since he stood to get most of the profits from the heist anyway.

So why had he been killed? And what was the diamond ring doing in his pocket?

I had wandered about three blocks by the time I looked up and noticed where I was. The Bayport Diner was on my right, making me realize how hungry I was. And on my left was a jewelry store with a sign that read EDMONDSON'S.

I remembered the guy from the morning before, who'd come in to certify the jewels as genuine. And something, some urge inside my head, made me go inside.

"Well, hello there!" said Nicholas Edmondson,

who'd been standing behind the counter, showing a fine jeweled watch to a customer. "I'll be with you in a moment, okay?"

I took a seat and waited for him to finish. When the customer left, Edmondson turned to me and said, "I remember you from yesterday morning. You're one of the security fellows from the convention center, aren't you?"

"Guilty as charged," I said, shaking his hand. "Frank Hardy."

"How can I help you, Frank? Is it about the robbery? I'm so shocked and appalled! Wasn't the place swarming with police?"

"It was. It was . . . a very sophisticated robbery, sir."

"Ah. Well, then. You wanted to see me about. . . ?"

"This," I said, pulling the ring out of my pocket and handing it to him.

"Ah, yes," he said, admiring it while holding it up to the light. "I remember this one. Lovely. I suppose they left it behind in their rush to get away?"

"I was just wondering," I said, ignoring his question. "Wasn't it you who was telling us about how the diamonds are etched with serial numbers to prove their authenticity?"

"I think that was Mr. Carrera." He sighed. "That poor man—I hope he was well insured."

"Didn't he say these had been etched with special

numbers to tie them to this specific batch of gems—you know, that were once illegal?"

"Yes, that's right."

"Well, could you look at this closely and write down the number for me? I think we could try and find the others that way."

"Certainly." He took the ring behind the counter and placed it on a viewing platform, then sat down and bent over his magnifier.

"Well?" I asked, ready with pen and paper to write the number down.

"But . . . this is impossible!" he gasped.

"What? What's impossible?"

"Where did you get this ring?"

"I—why? What do you see?"

"I see no number at all," he said.

"But I thought every diamond in the show had been specially etched!"

"Yes. But that's not all."

"No?"

"No. I'm afraid that stone is not a diamond at all—it's very good, mind you, but a fake is a fake. This," he said, handing it back to me, "is as phony as a three-dollar bill."

13.

Two Plus Two Is Sometimes Five

I called the police, and when they came, they took me into custody before I could even explain what happened. It took five hours before ATAC managed to convince them to let me go.

By the time I got back to Bayport, it was late afternoon. I found Frank alone at home, looking tired.

"Man," I said, "have I had a brutal day!" I proceeded to tell him everything I'd been through from the time I arrived in New York City.

When I was done, he looked even more troubled than before. I asked him why, and he told me about Shakey Twist's death, Bobo Hines's disappearance, and the fake diamond ring.

With all this new information, both of our heads

were reeling. We sat there in silence for a long time before Frank said, "Here's how I figure the whole thing went down."

"Shoot."

"See what you think of this scenario: Carlos Sanguillen arrives in the States from Antwerp a few days ago. He and Shakey already have plans in place to break into the convention center and steal the diamonds. Based on what we saw, I'd say their plan had to have been in the works for weeks, maybe months."

"Agreed," I said. "Go on."

"They have teams of technicians to replace the security camera tapes with cartoons, disable the laser motion-detection alarms and security systems, and make sure the escape route is clear while the 'A Team' goes in with their tanks full of knockout gas, their gas masks, their nail guns, and their hammers."

"Continue."

"They've got Sanguillen in the theater, watching the show to make sure everything's good on the inside. He leaves—we saw him go, remember?—and meets them backstage. The heist goes as planned, they get out with the gems and arrive at the dock, where the getaway boat is waiting for them."

"Good so far," I said. "What about Shakira?"

"What about her?"

"Didn't there have to be someone on the inside, helping? And remember, she dated Shakey till just a few months ago."

"Could be, but I don't see how she could have helped much. Maybe he got the idea for the heist because he knew about the upcoming show through her and decided to contact Sanguillen for muscle."

"Why couldn't he use his *own* muscle?"

"I don't know, maybe they're too well known to the police."

"Good point."

"And since the two guys who killed Glickstein were most likely Filipino, I think we can assume the 'A Team' was Sanguillen's men."

"Right."

"Besides, I doubt Shakey's own guys would have gunned him down on that dock."

"Right. Now, about that . . ."

"Here's how I make it out," Frank said. "They decide to check out the jewels—maybe to divide them right there, maybe just to get a look at them. I don't know. But they must have had a magnifier, because somebody realized the gems were fake. That's when the fight started, I'll bet—and it ended with Sanguillen or his guys taking down Twist and dumping him in the bay. Then, figuring Glickstein was the one who made the fakes for Shakey, they went to the city and killed him, too."

"Wait a minute," I said. "That's a crazy theory. Are you saying that between the time the diamonds were certified by Edmondson and the time the thieves broke into the center that night, the diamonds were switched for fakes that were made just for the occasion?"

"I know it sounds crazy, but, well . . . yes. That's exactly what I'm saying. It's the only thing that makes any sense."

I pondered this for a while, but I couldn't think of a better explanation. In fact, I couldn't think of *any* other explanation.

"Okay, then," I finally said, "so someone substituted the fakes for the real thing. But who? And how did they do it?"

"Let's start with the how," Frank said. "Remember, a lot of the protection systems were disabled by Sanguillen and Twist. Whoever substituted the fakes must have known the robbery was coming and pulled a double cross, figuring that Sanguillen and Twist would get blamed, while they themselves got away with the real goods."

"So who have we got for suspects?" I asked.

"They would have had to be inside the center during that day."

"Right. And they would have had to know about the robbery. And be ready with the fakes."

"I'll bet it was Glickstein who made them. He was into illegal activities up to his neck, and his name keeps popping up all over this thing."

"Okay," Frank said. "Let's see. Hal Harris knew a robbery might be coming."

"Too obvious," I said. "The head of security for the convention center? He'd be the first one they'd look at if there were suspicions of an inside job."

"Vincent Carrera?"

"Possibly. I'll try to get Chief Collig and Harris to get his alibi for that afternoon. But if you think about it, he would have been pretty busy. He was the one responsible for everything about the show going perfectly."

"True. I agree he's not a likely candidate, but definitely worth checking. How about Shakira and Naomi?"

"Are you nuts?" I said. "They're supermodels!"

"So? That makes them automatically innocent?"

"No, but come on—Naomi's got to be worth millions, and Shakira will be soon if she isn't already."

"You never know," Frank countered. "People lose fortunes amazingly fast sometimes. And you can never underestimate the power of greed—especially where diamonds are concerned."

"I guess . . ."

"And remember, Shakira dated Shakey not long ago. They supposedly broke up—but what if they didn't? She would have known about the upcoming heist and could have taken steps to double-cross him."

"But she didn't know Glickstein."

"How do you know?" he asked. "Maybe she met him through Twist."

He had a point. It was a definite possibility.

"What about Naomi, then?" I asked. "She has no mob connections."

"No? What about Bobo?"

"Bobo? He wasn't in the mob, was he?"

"He was in Sing Sing. With Twist. And Naomi says they hated each other. Maybe this was Bobo's way of getting even with Shakey."

"And now he's disappeared!" I said. "Frank, it fits!"

"We've got to find him, Joe. Either he's our man, and he's got the diamonds, or Sanguillen's caught up with him, and Bobo's already dead."

"Okay," I said. "Where do we start?"

"I guess at the hotel," Frank answered. "Maybe Naomi's got an idea where he might have gone. She's the only one left who knows him."

"Good plan," I said, and we were off. We hopped on our bikes and roared out of there, arriving at the hotel ten minutes later.

"We've got to speak with Naomi Dowd," Frank said to Officer Edwards, who was manning the front desk.

"Sorry, Frank," he said. "She left about ten minutes ago."

"She left?"

"Yeah—Chief said you asked us to finish up with her quickly."

"I did," he admitted. "But I didn't realize then— oh well, thanks anyway. Come on, Joe."

I bet Frank wanted to kick himself. If only he'd known the diamonds were fake, he'd never have told the chief to let her go. Between that and Bobo's disappearance, we really needed to talk to her now—she might hold the key to solving the case!

We emerged back out onto the street. The sun had just set, and the clouds were lit up in gorgeous colors over the bay, just like a painting. "Where to now?" I asked.

"I haven't got a clue, Joe." Just then, his cell phone chirped, and he flipped it open. "Hello? Naomi! Where are you?"

He listened, and his face grew dark with worry. "Are you sure the car's following you? Okay, okay, I believe you. Just . . . You pulled into the park? Oh, man. No, that probably wasn't a good idea—it's a dead end. . . . Wait—there's an old boathouse past the parking lot. If you can't drive out of the park because the entrance is covered, park your car off the road, behind some bushes or something, and hide in the boathouse till I get there. . . . I'll meet you there in five minutes."

"Jeez!" I said when he hung up. "What was that all about?"

"She's in her car, and she's being followed," he said. "You heard the rest."

"Why would they be following her?" I asked.

Frank sighed. "I'm not sure, Joe," he said. "But it's my job to protect her."

"I'm coming with you," I said.

"No. Not *with* me," he said. "I need you to alert Chief Collig. Tell him to send anyone he can spare. Then meet me there."

"Great plan, bro—*if* I don't get there too late."

"Leave that to me. I think I can handle myself for ten minutes."

I grinned. "Ah, yes, a man in love."

"Shut up," he said, and gave me a shove. But he couldn't hide the redness in his cheeks.

I just hoped he wasn't letting that crush get in the way of his good judgment.

FRANK

15.

Down by the Bay

I don't think I've ever ridden faster. It took me three minutes to get to Bayfront Park—record time. I pulled into the drive and cut the motor. My bike may be fast, but it's also really loud, and I didn't need to be announcing my arrival—so I reached into the bike's storage compartments, took a few items I thought might come in handy, and took off on foot toward the boathouse.

There was no doubt in my mind that Naomi was in deep trouble. The fear in her voice over the phone was all too real. I jogged down the road to the parking lot and hid behind a tree to check it out.

There were two cars in the lot. One was a red convertible with the top down. I could just see Naomi picking it out from the rental car lot. The other car, parked at a funny angle right behind it, was a slick-looking black sedan with tinted windows and a long radio antenna poking out of the trunk.

Just the kind of car a hit man would be driving.

I ran toward the old boathouse, keeping out of the light by hugging the trees at the edge of the parking lot.

The door to the boathouse was open. I'd known it would be. Months ago the place had been vandalized by a bunch of kids, and the town hadn't yet gotten around to fixing the broken lock.

I could hear a man's voice inside, speaking in low tones. And I could hear the loud breathing, mixed with frightened sobs, of a girl who wanted to stay alive.

"You're going to tell me, aren't you?" the heavily accented voice said. "Or do I have to ruin that perfect face of yours?"

"No! Please, no! I don't know what you're talking about!"

It was Naomi, all right.

"You'd better change your mind, girl, and tell me the truth."

"I am! I am telling the truth!"

"I don't think so," he growled. "You know they used to call me the butcher? You know why? Because I'm so good with a carving knife."

I wasn't going to wait around to find out what happened next. I picked up a short stick from the ground and stuck it into the pocket of my leather jacket. Then I took a deep breath and kicked the door open the rest of the way.

The inside of the boathouse was dark, the only light coming from the distant lamps along the riverside pathway, filtering in through the grimy windows.

In the center of the boathouse was a thick wooden pole the width of a decent-size tree trunk. It appeared to hold up the whole building. Strapped to the pole, with her hands tied behind her back, stood Naomi Dowd.

And facing her, standing with his shoulders hunched over as he recoiled from the surprise of my entrance, was Carlos Sanguillen, a huge knife in his hand. It glinted in the dim light, sharp and threatening.

"Freeze!" I shouted as loud as I could. My right hand was stuffed in my pocket, jabbing the stick into the leather so it looked—I hoped—like a gun. "Drop your weapon!"

Sanguillen slowly raised the hand with the knife. "You're making a big mistake," he snarled.

"Just drop it, okay?" I demanded.

"You do not use your head, my friend,"

Sanguillen said, turning the knife my way. "Lift the curtain from in front of your eyes, and see what is really happening!"

"I don't know what you're talking about," I said.

He spat on the ground and shook his head. "You don't want to see. You are blinded by beauty. You are nothing but a fool."

"Drop it, mister," I said as he took a step forward. "And stay right where you are!"

"Yes, a fool," he said, taking another slow step. "The kind of fool who pretends to have a gun when he really doesn't."

"You're mistaken," I said, standing my ground and trying to keep my legs from trembling. "Now back off!"

"I don't think I am mistaken." Another step. "Otherwise, show me the gun."

I laughed. More of a snort, really. "You're taking a big chance."

He smiled, showing me at least three gold teeth. "You are nothing but a boy. Yes, a boy in love. Ha!"

He flew at me, his knife raised. My hand came out of my pocket, the stick blocking his knife and snapping from the blow. With my left, I gave him a solid uppercut to the nose.

He reeled backward, bleeding from the nose and mouth, but he was still holding on to the knife.

"Okay, you worm," he said. "Now you die. You and she both."

He rose to his feet, and I waited for his next attack, bracing myself. Where in the world was Joe? Hadn't it been ten minutes by now? It felt like hours!

The knife whizzed through the air. I ducked to the left as his hand came down, then pulled on the knife arm and flipped him head over heels.

Amazingly, he was still holding onto the knife. Unfortunately for him, the sharp end was now sticking out of his back.

Yikes! I hadn't really meant things to work out like this.

"Is he dead?" Naomi asked in a trembling whisper as I bent over him, feeling his pulse.

"I'm afraid so."

"Oh, Frank, thank you! You saved my life!"

"I . . . guess I did," I said, backing away from the body.

"Untie me, quick!" she said. "There may be more of them coming!"

I took the razor I'd brought with me from the motorcycle and cut through the plastic handcuffs, freeing her.

"My hero," she said, throwing her arms around my neck and kissing me right on the lips.

Now my knees were really wobbling. I mean,

this was a dream come true, in a way. But on the other hand, there was Sanguillen, lying there, stone cold dead. And any minute, more of his men might show up.

I tried to untangle myself from her arms, but it wasn't easy.

At first I thought it was me—just so weak and stressed out by the fight. But no, it was Naomi— holding on to me, not letting go.

Was she that freaked out, I wondered? Or was she just crazy about me because I'd saved her life? The more I thought about it, the more it felt like she was, well, *trapping* me there.

I somehow got up the strength to pry her arms off of me. As I stepped back, I saw a black shape blocking the open doorway. The shape of a man.

A very big man.

I thought I recognized that hulking form. "Bobo?"

"Well, hello there, Mr. Bodyguard," he said, stepping forward into the dim light. Then he saw Sanguillen lying on the floor. "Nice work, buddy. Thanks for the help."

"The help?" I repeated. "Seems to me I didn't get any help from you."

"Like I said, thanks," he said. "Me and Naomi, we're very grateful."

"No problem. No hard feelings, then?" I asked,

thinking he was sticking out his hand to shake mine.

That's when I saw the gun.

"What the—?"

"Put your hands behind your back," he said. "Do it now."

I did as he said. "What do you think you're doing?"

"Surprised?" he said. "Not as stupid as I look, huh? Okay, Naomi, cuff him."

"I don't get it," I said. *"Naomi?"* She was already behind me, strapping a plastic cuff around my wrists.

"I'll explain later, once we're on the boat," she whispered in my ear as she shoved me forward. "Right now, we've got to get out of here."

It *had* to be ten minutes by now—where was Joe? If I could just stall them a little longer, I knew he'd show up, along with half the Bayport Police Department—

They must have known it too. That's why they were in such a hurry.

I dragged my feet. I stumbled and fell every chance I got. Bobo pistol-whipped me whenever I did that, but I didn't care—it was better than whatever else they had in mind for me.

In the distance I could hear the roar of Joe's bike. *Come on, Joe!*

They forced me down to the water, where a small speedboat was tied up. "Get on," Bobo said. "NOW!"

He shoved me over the rail, and I landed in a heap on the deck. Joe's engine was getting really loud now, but that also meant he wouldn't hear me if I cried out for help.

The bike's engine shut off. "JOE!" I yelled.

Bobo gunned the engine, and the boat lunged forward. Still lying on the deck, I rolled over toward the stern—and saw Joe appear at the shoreline.

Too late!

I felt Naomi's hands on my back. She helped me to sit up straight, then sat down next to me.

"Sorry about this, Frank," she said. "I feel bad about it. I mean, you just got through saving my life, and now, well . . ."

"You're going to kill me, aren't you." It was a statement, not a question.

She didn't answer yes or no. Instead, she said, "I feel I owe you a full explanation."

"Good," I said. "I'd like that."

"You see, Bobo and I—well, this is a big secret—we're going to get married. Next week—in Paraguay."

"Paraguay?"

"It's this country in South America where they don't send you back to the States to face trial."

"You're the ones who switched the fake diamonds for the real ones!" I said, feeling like a complete idiot.

She smiled and nodded. "Pretty brilliant, huh? We found out Shakey and Sanguillen were going to steal them, and we worked out how to make them take the blame, while we got away with the real diamonds!"

Bobo was steering us straight out into the heart of the bay, far from anything. I began to see what they had in store for me: a watery grave. Then they'd continue out, into open water. Somewhere out there, a bigger boat was waiting for them, one they could ride clear to South America.

"When you and Joe showed up at the convention center, at first I thought it was going to mess everything up," Naomi said. "If you'd been able to stop Shakey and Sanguillen from stealing the fakes, it would have ruined the whole plan. Luckily, you didn't."

"Yeah. That was real lucky," I said, wishing I could get that razor blade back out of my pocket and cut my cuffs off. "How did you pull the switch?" I asked. "Just curious."

"That was the beauty part," she said. "We knew Sanguillen and Shakey would be messing with the alarms and the security systems. So they wouldn't be working right when Bobo switched them."

"How did he open the cases?"

"He waited till the motion sensors went dead.

Then he just lifted the cases up and took the diamonds."

"But—"

"Remember when I sent him to get my iPod? Remember how long he was gone?"

I *did* remember, come to think of it. So *that* was when he switched the gems!

"Who made the fakes for you?"

"Glickstein," she said.

"Of course! And that's why they killed Glickstein when they found out the gems were fake!"

"Uh-huh. He was supposed to get a share of the money afterward—but Bobo and I figured the others would take care of that for us. And they did! The poor man . . .

"We knew once Shakey and Sanguillen found out the gems had been switched, they'd hit the ceiling. One would surely kill the other, and then, thinking Glickstein had double-crossed him, the survivor would pay him a little visit. And thanks to you, Frank, we don't have to worry about Sanguillen anymore."

She leaned over and kissed me on the forehead. "You're such a sweetheart. And this is going to be so hard for me. . . ."

That's when Bobo cut the engine. "Okay," he said, letting go of the rudder and coming toward me. "Let's get this thing done."

JOE

16.
The Chase Is On

I got to the boathouse just a little too late, and you know what they say—a miss is as good as a mile. I ran straight down to the waterside, in time to see the boat pull away from the shore, with my brother on it.

I knew that if I didn't want it to be his last ride, I'd better get after them somehow.

I looked around. There were a couple dozen boats moored by the dock at the water's edge, but only one of them looked fast enough to catch the boat Frank was on. I hopped aboard and started hot-wiring it.

I know, I know, stealing a boat is against the law. But at that moment, I didn't have much of a choice. Later on ATAC would have to reimburse the owner for gas . . . and whatever damage I wound up doing.

It only took me a minute or so to get the motor running. I cast off and headed out after them, pedal to the metal in the direction I thought they'd gone (it was hard to tell in the darkness).

It was a pretty cool boat, I have to say. Way faster than any I'd ever been on before. They'd gotten a big head start on me, but after two or three minutes, just when I thought I'd lost them, I spotted their wake far ahead of me, lit by the light of the rising full moon.

Two or three minutes later, I was close enough to see people on board. Three people, it looked like. And they were getting closer every second.

I realized they'd cut their engine and were coming to a stop, because I was gaining on them quickly now. Then one of them seemed to see me, because he panicked and headed back to the wheel. A big guy—I thought I recognized him as Bobo Hines. I was surprised, but only mildly. Whoever it was, I was going to have to deal with him if I wanted to save my brother.

Just as I was slowing down, about to come alongside, the other boat pulled away again.

Soon we were both going full speed, side by side. Every few seconds the other boat veered away to the left, away from me. I'd veer over too, but then it would veer left again. We were soon going around in circles, side by side.

I could see them perfectly now—Bobo at the

wheel, with Naomi leaning over the stern, heaving her guts up every time he made a sharp left.

But where was Frank?

I figured he must have been down on the deck, tied up. Otherwise, he'd have been up there like before. The boat's motion must have thrown him down when it kicked into gear.

We were just a few feet apart now. One false move, and the two boats would smack into each other. If that happened, we'd all die out here.

Suddenly, I saw Bobo turn toward me and level a gun.

BAM!

I ducked, just as the bullet whizzed by.

He was a pretty good shot. I mean, we were both speeding in circles, bouncing up and down on each other's wakes, and he only missed me by inches.

The second shot was even closer. If this kept up, I was going to get hit with the next shot, or the one after that. I knew I had to do something to change the odds.

So I did. Taking off my leather jacket, I stuffed it in between the wheel and its housing, so my boat wouldn't change course. Then, without warning, I ran to the rail and leaped over, landing on the other boat.

I did a somersault roll and came up right in front

of Bobo. He looked frozen in surprise, which was a good thing. Because before he could level his gun at me, I had a hand on his firing arm, forcing it away from me.

He fired twice more as I banged his arm down on the gunwale. The third whack separated the gun from his hand. It slid down the deck, away from us and toward Naomi.

She saw it and tried to reach for it, with one hand holding on to the rail for dear life—but it slid just out of her reach, straight through one of the gaps in the railing, and into the bay.

Well, that was a good thing. But Bobo's stranglehold on my neck was not so good.

Lucky for me, Frank somehow managed to free his hands, just in time to deal Bobo a swift karate chop to the back of the neck. He crumpled, and I could breathe again—not a moment too soon, either, because I was already seeing stars, and they weren't the ones in the sky.

Frank slowed the boat down to a crawl. The other boat kept going around in speedy circles. It would probably keep going till it ran out of gas. I sure hoped it wouldn't slam into anything—like us, for instance.

Bobo had gotten to his feet again, and I could see from the look in his eyes that he wasn't done with us yet. He fished a knife from his belt and waved it in front of him.

"Frank?" I said.

"On three," he replied. "One . . . two . . ."

He never got to three. Bobo rushed at me, waving the knife. I ducked, grabbing his leg and flipping him. Then Frank stomped on the arm with the knife, separating it from his grasp.

Bobo was strong, all right. It took both of us to lift him into the air and throw him overboard.

"Bobo!" Naomi screamed, climbing onto the railing and making like she wanted to jump ship and join him. "Help me!"

"I can't!" he yelled back. "I can't swim!"

"Better throw him a life preserver," Frank said.

I fished one out and threw it overboard, while Frank got hold of Naomi and made her climb back down onto the deck.

"I guess we'd better haul him out," I said.

"Sure thing," Frank agreed, going to the wheel and steering us over next to Bobo.

In the distance I saw bright searchlights coming toward us. "Nice," I said. "That'd be Chief Collig's port patrol unit, just in time."

"Actually," Frank said, "we could've used them ten minutes ago."

"Oh, well," I said. "Better late than never."

I went over to Naomi, who had crumpled in a heap and was crying. "Well, Frank," I said, "I guess it's true what they say—beauty is only skin deep."

17.

When Love Comes Calling

We were sitting in the kitchen, Joe and I, reading through the Bayport papers, cutting out all the articles about the heist. The headlines read: BAYPORT POLICE BREAK BIG CASE; SUPERMODEL, BODYGUARD HELD IN DIAMOND SWITCH.

Another paper featured a series of mug shots: Shakey Twist, Carlos Sanguillen, Bobo Hines, and Naomi Dowd. There were red Xs through Shakey's and Sanguillen's photos, indicating that they were dead. FOUR BIRDS WITH ONE STONE, the headline read. Underneath was a photo of the mayor pinning a medal on Chief Collig, with the caption: "Man of the hour."

"Can you believe this?" Joe asked, showing it to me. "That is so bogus!"

"Never mind, Joe," I said. "We don't want the publicity. You know how ATAC protects its secrecy."

"I guess," he said, frowning. "I just hate to see Chief Collig grab all the credit."

"That was probably the mayor's doing," I said. "The chief's a good guy, you know that."

"I guess," he said again. Then, "You know what really burns me?"

"What?"

"We never got to date the girls."

"Well, in my case, that's probably a good thing," I said. "She may not have been a murderer, but she knew people would die if her scheme succeeded, and she went along with it, all the way."

"Well, that's you. What about me, huh?"

I shrugged. "If you feel that badly about it, why don't you give Shakira a call?"

His eyes brightened. "Hey, that's right—she gave me her cell number! Now, where did I put it. . . ?"

He started fishing through his pockets.

"Joe, I was just kidding," I said.

"Whatever—I'm gonna call her, man." He pulled a crumpled business card out of his pocket. "Here it is!" He fished out his cell phone and started dialing.

"Joe, forget her, man. Let's just move on, okay?"

"Yeah, right—*you* move on, bro. I'm movin' *in*."

He listened for a minute, then said, "Shakira? It's Joe! How're you doin'?"

He listened again. "Joe Hardy. You know, your bodyguard? In Bayport? At the show?"

He listened again, his smile fading. "Well, you said to call you if I wanted to get in touch with you. . . . Yeah, I know you meant during the diamond show, but I thought . . ."

Joe looked like he'd been slapped in the face. "But you said . . . yeah, I know the papers didn't mention us, but . . . but . . ."

He held the phone away from his ear, shaking his head. "She hung up on me! Can you believe that?"

"What'd she say?"

"She didn't see my name mentioned in any of the papers, so I'm still a nobody to her!"

"Man, that really bites."

"Yeah."

"Forget about it," I said. "Remember what you told me back on that boat?"

"No. What?"

"You said, 'Beauty is only skin deep.'"

"Did I say that?"

"Uh-huh."

"What was I thinking?"

"You were right," I said. "It's personality that counts in the end."

He sighed and put his cell phone back in his pocket. "I guess you're right. She sure was fine, though, wasn't she?"

"They both were."

"Man, I'm never gonna let myself fall for somebody like that again."

"Me neither," I agreed.

"So . . . what's next?"

"Uh . . . how about school? It starts in twenty minutes."

And so it was. Everyday life strikes again. Yesterday we'd been this close to being famous. Today we were back to being just us—a couple of average guys, with a secret identity that was doomed to remain secret.

Joe got up from his chair, groaning like an old man. "Oh, well," he said with a sigh. "Easy come, easy go."